Chronicles From Château Moines

EVELYNE HOLINGUE

Visit our website at evelyneholingue.com

Cover design by Jennifer Zemanek

ISBN: 0988390515
ISBN-13: 978-0988390515 (Burel Press)

For my children who did not grow up in France.

CONTENTS

1   AN AMERICAN IN CHÂTEAU MOINES

[Sylvie, September 14, 1970:]

My mother's smiling face appears next to mine in the mirror.

"You look so pretty," she says, fluffing the balloon sleeve of my shirt. "Perfect!" she adds with a nod.

But the girl in the mirror doesn't look perfect to me, and the words of a new song play in my head.

Homemade food tastes great.
But who likes homemade jeans?
If only my father's truck
Could bring me the Levi's of my dreams
It might change my look.
But no such luck. I'm stuck
Wearing homemade, mother-made jeans.

I pull on my shirt and then tuck it in. "Maman, the jeans aren't real."

Chocolat, my Labrador, licks my hand and drops at my feet, peeking at my reflection through his sleepy eyes.

Maman drops her hand from my shoulder. "Sylvie, we already spoke about this."

Chocolat opens a lazy eye and points his ears. I avoid the green eyes of the girl in in the mirror as I say, "Maman, people don't make their own jeans."

"Don't you like wearing unique clothes?"

"Once in a while I'd like to get something from a store." Besides the jeans, I also wish for a camouflage bag. Maman said the bag is not feminine and is too small to hold more than one textbook. So I'm carrying my old brown vinyl satchel.

"Listen," Maman says. "When your father comes back, I can buy new fabric and—"

"I won't wear another pair of homemade pants."

Maman steps to the window. "Then you won't," she says, her back turned to me.

I catch the disappointment and hurt in her voice. I know she's a skilled seamstress; nobody has ever made fun of my clothes. I don't want to hurt her feelings, but truth is I'm embarrassed to wear homemade clothes now that I am starting seventh grade.

Maman draws the curtains wide open. Sun pours inside La Boutique. La Boutique is in fact the dining room, but since we always eat in the kitchen and never have anyone but Mémé, Maman's mother, for dinner, this is where Maman sews and welcomes her brides-to-be. Also, this room is the only one in my home to have a wall-to-wall mirror, and I use it in the morning to check my outfit and brush my long hair.

A tiny hand wraps around my wrist. "Sylvie! We've got to go!"

In the tall mirror, I see that the big smile of my little sister Elle matches the beautiful weather. She just can't wait to show off her new yellow dress, even though it's also homemade. Maman squeezes between Elle and me. She throws her arms around our shoulders.

"My little girls," she says. "You are just perfect."

"We'll be late," I say.

Maman plants a good-bye kiss on Elle's cheek. "*Au revoir, mon cœur.*"

"*Au revoir,* Maman." Elle saunters away.

Maman kisses the top of my head. "*Au revoir, mon chou.*"

I'm a little bit too big to be called a *chou*, a puff pastry, but I say *au revoir* anyway.

Chocolat follows us to the door and pokes his head outside. Maman nudges him back with a gentle heel. "Dogs don't go to school," she says, and she closes the door behind us.

The streets are filled with boys and girls carrying bags and backpacks. Cars honk at the bikes swerving between them. Château Moines smells of back-to-school day.

"Hurry up!" Elle pulls my hand. "I want to see my friends."

The only face that I am looking forward to seeing that early in the morning is Annie's. Just then, someone slaps my back. I wheel around. Annie grins at me, grabs my arm, and, in a rushed voice, says, "There's a new boy in town!"

"*Bonjour* to you too," I say. "Really?"

"Really." Annie lets go of my arm. "His family moved in two days ago into the apartment above the empty store, and he came into the bakery. I didn't help him, but I had plenty of time to watch him." She covers her mouth with her hand, but excitement flickers in her eyes. "He's very cute and he speaks funny! I wonder where he's from. He looks our age. Imagine if he's in our class!"

Nobody moves away from the town of Château Moines. Nobody moves to Château Moines either. Annie is an exception. I had never met a foster girl before she arrived three years ago. So I have a hard time imagining the new boy.

We drop Elle at the gates of the elementary school. Annie hurries ahead to our school and I tag along. We climb the few steps that lead to the seventh-grade class, and Annie inspects the students' list taped on the door.

"Check," she says as she matches the names on the list to the students who pass us by. "Check, check, check." Her finger freezes. "Here! I found him. *Scott Sweet.*"

In deliciously accented French, a voice echoes Annie's exaggerated British accent, "*Bonjour.*"

I turn around, and a song title jumps to my shocked brain: "Lost in Château Moines." Because if

12

the boy I see isn't lost, what is he doing here?

His faded bell-bottom Levi's hug his hips, and a turquoise T-shirt matches his eyes. I've never been south of France, but Papa has sent me postcards. This boy's eyes rival the color of the Mediterranean Sea. He doesn't wear any socks with his Indian-style sandals. He's got a perfectly worn-out army bag with buttons and badges. I recognize the peace sign and the names of big American cities, which make me feel small and ignorant. A pair of roller skates is tied to the straps of his bag. With his shaggy haircut, he belongs more in *Mademoiselle* magazine than in Château Moines middle school. I must have looked as stunned as Saint Bernadette when she saw the Virgin Mary in Lourdes, because Scott points at his chest.

"*Je suis* Scott Sweet," he says with the same exotic accent.

"*Non, non.*" Annie switches to a patient tone. "In French, you say: '*Je m'appelle* Scott Sweet.'"

Scott flashes a Paul Newman smile. "Juh mahpell Scott Sweet," he repeats.

I'm positive that I am hallucinating, but when I peek, the new boy is standing one meter away from me. A nice but strange smell wafts to my nose.

I must have flared my nostrils, because Scott says, "Patchouli."

Despite his smile, he looks confused, and I wonder how it feels to be the new kid at school and to be a foreigner.

Annie turns to me and clasps her hands together.

"We have a new boy at school," she says. "And he speaks French with an American accent! *J'adore!*"

I don't adore Annie at all right now, but I can't blame her. She saw him first at the bakery. Then she found his name on the list. *And* she can speak some English.

For some reason, I have the feeling that this first day of school marks the beginning of a lot of unpleasant firsts.

2 PHANTOMS OF THE PAST

[*Scott:*]

My sister Stacey pokes her head through my bedroom door. "Hey," she says.

"Isn't Dad home?" I growl. My head pounds after this first day of school, and I would give just about any of my favorite records to Stacey if she would leave me alone.

She cocks her head like a sad-looking puppy. "Not yet."

I sigh. "Come on in."

Stacey smiles the great smile that she inherited from Mom and plops down right next to me.

"Hey!" I say. "Move over!"

Stacey cuddles closer. "My first day was far out! I made tons of friends!" She lists them on the tip of her fingers. "Dominique, Paul, *and* I also made a best friend. Her name is Christelle, but everyone calls her Elle."

I zone out while she recites her list. I'm thinking that Mom would be happy to know that Stacey is excited. One of her biggest worries on the first day of school wasn't about the teachers we got, but about the friends we made. I don't feel like asking Stacey how she managed to remember all these names when I didn't memorize a single one. And I don't ask her how she could talk to everybody while I spent the entire day pretending I understood everything. My brain feels like a big bag stuffed with names, words, and sentences, all in French. Thanks to Mom, I knew enough French to fool the kids, yet they watched me as if I were an alien that Neil Armstrong brought back from the moon. My clothes and roller skates gave me away before I opened my mouth.

Stacey taps on my arm. "Are you listening?"

"Huh?"

"I said Paul is very small," she says right in my face. "We call him 'petit Paul.'" She blushes and lowers her tone. "I think he is in love with me."

I roll my eyes. "Come on, you're eight years old!"

Stacey shoots her eyebrows up. "So? Anyway my school is really cool."

"If you say so."

I stand up and put an old Beach Boys record on my player. "Surfin' USA" takes me home to when Mom was healthy. I feel for her earring in my pocket, and my hand seals around it. It gets as warm as if it were alive.

"Did you make friends too?" Stacey's voice hauls me back from my memories.

"Uh, uh." Although the school is a million times smaller than mine back home, the faces I saw today blend together like the pieces of an unfinished puzzle. In the mass, I only noticed a boy, looking as displaced as me, with his dark skin and tight black curls. "But I will make friends," I say, when I catch Stacey observing me.

"Hey," she says. "The fabric looks cool on the wall."

I didn't thank Mom when she brought me this gift from France. She told me it was a copy from a medieval tapestry. Then I couldn't have cared less about the musical scene embroidered on the fabric. She had left us for two weeks and I was pretty angry. Besides taking care of myself, I had to watch over Stacey after school and clean the house, since Dad taught private art lessons in addition to his full-time art teacher job. He said we needed extra money for Mom's treatments and her trip. Although I know she had little time left, I'm still upset that she chose to be alone rather than being with us, and once in a while, I wonder why it was so important for her to go to France then, when we never even went together.

The song is over, and Stacey asks if I want to watch TV. Before I agree, she has jumped from my bed and run to the living room.

The TV sits on the floor, next to a pile of empty boxes stamped with all kinds of customs seals in French and English. On the one hand they are depressing; on the other hand they give me hope. Perhaps if Dad has kept the boxes we won't stay after all. I will go back to Santa Monica and have a soda at the Sunny Shake with Mike and Pete before catching the bus home. On Saturday we'll go to the movies, and on Sunday we'll play baseball on the field behind Pete's house. His brother Jake will cheer for us from his wheelchair. I'll avoid looking at his empty left pants leg flapping in the wind. Pete says that soon Jake will get something that will be almost like a real leg.

How long do you have to wait for a leg?

"Are you okay?" Stacey's small face is pinched with concern.

"Groovy," I say, and we drop to the floor, leaning our backs against the base of the sofa.

Stacey turns the TV on. "What did they say?" she asks every few seconds.

I give her a little tap on top of the head. "They say Stacey should shut up and watch."

Stacey sighs. "Very funny. I wish I could watch *The Brady Bunch*."

I miss my shows, too. Plus they only have two channels here. "Sorry. We aren't in Santa Monica anymore."

"I know that," Stacey says.

I notice how her voice cracks just a little. "I feel bad we had to leave," I say. Stacey lets me take her hand. Both of hers could fit in one of mine.

"We agreed to come here," she says, back to her upbeat voice, "because Daddy said France had been good to him."

"Talking about me?" Dad's voice jolts us. He

stands in the doorway, wearing his frayed jeans as if he was on the boardwalk. Hasn't he realized that he's the only man his age to wear jeans here? And I haven't seen any men with ponytails either.

"Daddy!" Stacey leaps to her feet.

"How are you, my favorite daughter?" he croons.

"Daddy, I'm your only one!"

"Right!" My father hugs her tight and asks me how my day was.

"Okay, I suppose."

"Made some friends?"

"In one day?"

"I did! I did!" Stacey says. She tells Dad about her friends and her best friend, and the boy she thinks loves her.

The whole time I wonder why Dad ever believed we'd feel better 6,000 miles away from home.

"How do you like your new school?" Dad asks me.

"Perfect," I say through my teeth.

Dad gives a squeeze to my shoulder. "It takes time to settle in a new country, but I have plenty of ideas."

I push his hand back. "Sure. Like art lessons for French kids?"

"Stacey, honey, can you get me a glass of water, please?"

Stacey runs to the kitchen, using her socks as roller skates.

"Listen," Dad says, looking me straight in the eye. "I know it's hard. But I had to." He runs his hand through his ponytail, and I spot some gray I never saw before. "I'll tell you more soon. Give me just a little time and, trust me, our business will thrive." He smiles, but I also notice a bunch of wrinkles across his forehead.

"I don't know what you have in mind, Dad. But no offense, do you think an American business can work in France? I mean there are so many French here!"

Dad laughs and his face relaxes. "That's a funny one!"

"What's funny, Daddy?" Stacey asks, handing him a glass of water.

"Hey!" Dad says. "What if we had dinner out tonight?"

"On a school day?" Stacey exclaims. "Mom won't—"

She stops mid-sentence, and the three of us wait for the phantoms of our past to disappear.

3 RADIO CHÂTEAU MOINES

[*Sylvie:*]

I was so right. Too many new things are happening, and I am the foreigner in my familiar school.

First of all, since no words in English or French come to my mind whenever Scott is nearby, I'm the only one who hasn't spoken to him yet. Then, for the fifth day in a row, as I drop my satchel two seats behind him, I can't help staring at Brigitte as she plops her perfect derriere on the very same bench as Scott. She just inspired me for the beginning of a new song.

In my pair of flared jeans and platform shoes
My white sweater tight as a sock
With my blonde hair that licks my shoulders
I'm a Parisian stuck in Château Moines.

Annie catches my stare and leans in to me. "Who said life was fair?" she whispers.

Fortunately, the clearing of a familiar raspy voice stirs me away from the unfairness of life. *"Bonjour, mes enfants."* For Monsieur Leroy, we are his children. And he is so nice that I wouldn't mind having him for an uncle. He teaches French and Latin, my best subjects.

"I know," Monsieur Leroy says. "First week of school is hard. But it will get better. It can't be worse, can it?" His beat-up satchel lands with a thump on his desk.

He surveys the classroom like a border collie watching over his herd, and waves at Scott. "Scott," he says. "I've already noticed that your French is quite good."

"Comme çi, comme ça," Scott says.

I can't help the cramping in my belly when he turns to Brigitte and his tan face breaks into an apologetic smile.

"You'll be fine," Monsieur Leroy says in a reassuring voice. "Just a little bit of help could give you the boost you need to be fluent by the end of the year. What do you say?"

"In grammar, maybe," Scott says. "And spelling and—"

"I can help!" Brigitte and Annie snap up from their seats like two elastic bands.

"Sit down!" I hiss to Annie, and the words of a song I don't like at all bud inside me: "American Dream Boy Jeopardizes Peace in Château Moines."

With Brigitte batting her eyelashes whenever Scott looks at her, Annie craning her neck whenever he opens his mouth, and the rest of the class acting like we have a movie star at school, my last day of the week is by far the worst. So I'm not in the best mood when I get Elle at her school.

"Stacey says she has a brother," she says, trotting behind me. "Is he in your class? Does he speak English too?"

I pick up my pace to distance myself from her questions. Besides, the sound of her satchel slamming against her back irritates me, as it reminds me of my old one.

"Wait for me!" Elle says. Her breathing comes fast, right behind me.

"It's not my fault if your legs are short," I say.

"My legs aren't short!"

"Yes, they are!"

"What's wrong with you?" Elle has caught up with me.

Words bang against my skull and I take off, impatient to get them down in my notebook. I slam my body into the front door, which bursts open. Chocolat wags his tail like a flag on Bastille Day.

"Get away!" I hiss. He blinks his eyes and tucks his tail between his legs. "Sorry," I say. I scratch his head and he sighs, licking my free hand.

The radio hums from the kitchen and I catch a few notes of "Mrs. Robinson." Why do even Simon and Garfunkel remind me of Scott?

Maman sticks her head out the door of La Boutique. She holds a pin between her fingers. A

23

dozen more are planted in a cushion above her wrist. "*Bonjour, mon chou,*" she says with a wave in my direction. "I'm busy with last touches on Florence's wedding dress." She disappears inside, but leaves the door ajar.

Florence is posing in front of the mirror. Meters of white silk and tulle flow to the floor. Maman gets to her knees and starts to hem the gown.

With a twist of my shoulders, I get rid of my satchel, which slumps on the floor. I attack the stairs two at a time.

"Shoes!" Maman calls.

They tumble downstairs and thump onto the shoe mat. I close the door of the room I share with Elle. My record player sits on my desk, and I put the latest Carole King on, but today I can't stand her American accent, which reminds me of Scott's. I switch to Françoise Hardy, my all-time French favorite singer. Her voice makes me dream of Paris and sophisticated places.

I pull out my trunk from underneath my bed. I flip my notebook open to the last page I wrote. Words rush, annoying and unnerving, like my heart when I think of Scott.

I hate you and I like you.
You change my world.
But my world is mine.
Your name is poetic.
You come from California.
But I should care less about

Your patchouli smell and your ridiculous "bonzhoor."

Writing usually makes my thoughts more clear and calms my fears, but today is different. The record crackles, and the last line of a song repeats, like my thoughts, which keep returning to Scott.

Maman's footsteps on the stairs make me jump. I tuck my notebook under my pillow and push my trunk under my bed, just before Maman pushes the door open. White threads cling to her dress.

"Where's Elle?" she says, looking around.

"On her way." I rearrange my bedcover so it falls to the floor.

"What?" Maman's voice catches in her throat. "You can't leave her like that!"

"She is slower than a snail!"

Maman throws her hands up. "What's wrong with you?"

"Nothing! Leave me alone!"

"I want you downstairs. Now! And turn your music off!" She slams the door after a loud "*Nom d'un chien!*"

Maman never swears. True, swearing on the name of a dog is not quite the same as the expletives Papa uses when he fixes the old Peugeot or is angry at his truck. Still.

Elle is in the kitchen by the time Maman and I reach the bottom of the stairs. "Maman! Sylvie didn't wait for me. She left me all alone. Plus there was tons of traffic."

Maman smoothes a strand of Elle's hair and

pushes it back behind her ear. "Are you all right, *mon cœur?*"

"I was so scared," Elle says in a whiny voice. But behind our mother's back she shoots me a victorious glare.

Maman turns toward me. "Elle is only eight."

"And one quarter," Elle pipes up.

"Sylvie, you are the oldest," Maman goes on. "You have to protect your sister." She gives me a small smile. "Besides I need your help when your father's on the road. He won't be back for a few more days." She flattens her dress with both hands.

Elle perks up her ears. "Why is he gone so long?"

"Don't worry, he's fine. I just don't need your arguing when I'm alone."

"I get it," I say, realizing that, although I'd like to see my father, I'm also getting used to his long absences. I slide onto a chair. The cold of the Formica goes through the denim of my homemade jeans. Another American song plays on the radio, and I crank the volume down.

"I like that song." Elle reaches for the radio.

I bring my hand to her wrist. "I don't."

Elle sits across from me. Her hair flies around her flushed cheeks; she has run all the way home.

"You want to play Mille Bornes?" I ask.

She springs from her chair and dashes to the hallway closet, a cookie stuck between her teeth. She returns with the card game.

"I meant when I'm finished with my homework."

I crank the radio up a notch higher. Joe Dassin's deep and warm voice fills the kitchen with the number-one song in France now: "L'Amérique." If that's not conspiracy, then what is?

Maman pours some steaming milk into our cups of cocoa, and pulls up a chair next to me. "Sylvie, you have to watch over Elle."

I nod, and Maman hands me the tin of cookies. I can see that she is as relieved as I am that a cookie has saved us from an argument.

"Can I go play outside?" Elle asks when the kitchen has turned silent.

"Go," Maman says. "But stay in the yard." She waits for the door to close behind Elle, and she brings her chair closer to mine. "I heard there is a new boy at school."

In Château Moines, news travel as fast as the recently launched Concorde airplane. If only the fastest plane on earth could fly Scott Sweet back to California!

Maman sips her cocoa as if, now that I have promised to watch over Elle, we can enjoy a nice social time. "Tell me, *mon chou*," she says. "Is this boy nice?"

"He doesn't even speak French."

"Mémé told me that an American family moved in town," Maman says. She picks at the threads on her dress. "What are Americans doing here?"

I'm sure my grandmother will know the answer before I get to say one word to Scott Sweet. That plants the seeds for new lyrics: "Hollywood Star in Alien Land." The problem is, when I think of Scott and how he has blended among us, I wonder who the alien is.

4 THE OTHER SIDE OF CHÂTEAU MOINES

[*Scott, September 20, 1970:*]

Our house in Santa Monica had a view of the ocean. Now we live above an empty store in an old apartment. It has a fireplace in each room, but only one bathroom, with a weird tub. Dad says, "How can you not love an authentic white claw-footed tub?" I miss my shower stall. Fortunately, the French have separate rooms for the toilets, and although ours is no bigger than a closet, I can at least be alone for my personal business. Dad let me pick my room, and I chose the one with the French windows that open on a balcony. I can look out over a huge forest that spreads beyond the town.

Today is Saturday. I'm only now unpacking the boxes that have been piled in my room since we arrived. I stack my records against the wall. My record player fits right on top of the mantelpiece. The apartment has been unoccupied for many years and smells like wet mushrooms. I light a stick of incense, and the scent spirals through my room.

One by one I unroll my posters, and my life from before jumps to my eyes, but the familiar faces of the Beatles, Janis Joplin, Chicago, and Simon and Garfunkel can't bring my real life back. I pin Janis above my bed, pushing the tacks in so hard it hurts my thumb.

I dig in another box and find my baseball and mitt. Besides the soccer field downtown I haven't seen any sports field around, so I hook my Dodgers cap around the doorknob and stick the bat in a corner of my room.

I trail my fingers along my guitar. Dust flies away, catching the light. I haven't played since Mom's death. Everyone had a guitar back home, so Mom took me to the store to pick one I liked. After Mom died I wanted to give it away, but Dad said I would regret it. Maybe he's right; now that I am so far from home, now that Mom has been dead for six months and I don't have anything to do, I should give music another try.

A knock at my door makes me jump. "Only me," Dad says, poking his head in. "It's beautiful outside. Why don't you go explore? Stacey needs some help with her homework, so you can be on your own for once."

I appreciate that Dad realizes how we are always together since we arrived in France. When I open my window, the sun and wind fill my room, and I agree that unpacking can wait.

"I heard the public library is stellar," Dad says. "Might want to check it out."

"Enough books for now," I say, pointing to the boxes piled in a corner.

Dad enters my room. "You'll need to switch to French, you know that?"

"What about you?"

"Oh, it's a bit different for me. I'm fluent."

"Fluent?" I say with a laugh. "Like talking in half French, half English?"

"Let's say that I can manage." Dad rubs his chin.

"Really? Like with the school registration? I was the one who gave you the pen after the principal asked you twice to sign the paperwork."

Dad laughs, and his laugh flies me back to Santa Monica, but I don't want to go there so I say, "See you later."

I grab my army jacket, the one with the signatures of the people I met at the peace rallies. I went to many sit-ins and marches to protest the Vietnam War. Although Mom was sick with cancer and tired, she wanted us to go to the big march in Washington, DC, last November. A half million protesters poured into the city. I went for Jake. He won't ever play basketball the way he did. The war took his leg and killed his dream. Although the march was huge, we haven't stopped the war yet. I wonder if it will ever end.

I push the heavy door that opens onto Main

Street. In French, that is "rue Principale." Our apartment sits between a flower shop and a cobbler's shop. Further down the street, there is a bakery and a butcher shop, a deli and a grocery store. There is also a pharmacy, another bakery, and a boutique that only sells tea, pastries, and ice cream. The French call it a *salon de thé*. I've only seen old women there.

The café Chez Lili stands at the corner. It smells of coffee and tobacco whenever I walk by. Today, the laughter of people playing pinball and a French song reach me. I feel around my pocket. Besides Mom's earring, I find a few francs. Maybe I could check out the jukebox and get a soda.

Smoke stings my eyes when I enter the café. "*Bonjour*," I say, although I know it sounds more like *bonzhoor*.

Men at the bar turn at once toward me and stop talking. A collection of military medals hangs on the jacket of one. Another one wears a black felt hat that shades his eyes. A cigarette dangles from the corner of his mouth.

"What can I do for you?" The waiter stands behind the counter, arms crossed on his chest. Several framed pictures stand on a shelf behind him. Each one is of a woman and a little girl, smiling at whoever is taking their picture.

"*Un soda, s'il vous plaît?*" I ask in my most polite and best French.

Silence follows my request. The waiter furrows his brow. "Excuse me?" he finally says.

A few more men gather around me. The jukebox now plays "Let It Be," and the English language sounds so beautiful and so reassuring to my ears.

"*Un soda, s'il vous plaît,*" I say, articulating each word.

The waiter turns toward the man with the medals. "Do you get that, Colonel?"

"*Pfft,*" the Colonel says with a shrug.

The waiter returns to drying his glasses, but the men observe me like the kids at school do sometimes, as if I were a moon rock.

"*Un* Coca," a voice says from the back. The dribbling of a soccer ball accompanies his words. I recognize Ibrahim, the soccer star, and the only kid with dark skin in my class. "He said he'd like a Coca-Cola."

"That's not what he said." The waiter hangs the glasses on the racks, above the pictures.

"Come on, Garçon." Ibrahim rolls his ball between his feet. "He's new in town. Give him a break."

The waiter leans over the bar. "Don't give me any lessons, will you? Also, my café isn't a soccer field."

An exchange in fast French follows. I miss many words but I understand that the bartender's nickname is Garçon, which is how the French call the waiter in a café. I also pick up a few swear words, but a bottle of Coca-Cola appears on the counter. The white logo looks like an old friend. I put my money down and grab the cool bottle by its neck.

"Don't forget the tip, *l'américain*," Garçon says, loud and clear.

Laughter erupts, and I drop an extra franc before rushing out with my drink, with Ibrahim on my heels.

"*Merci*," I say, when we are back on the sunny sidewalk.

I take his "*Bah*" for a "you're welcome." He taps the ball onto the ground. "Next time," he says, jerking a thumb at the café, "leave only a few centimes for the tip."

I feel myself blushing. With a mother from France, I should know much more about this country. But I've never been here before. Mom kept postponing our trip, because Stacey was too young, because Dad had started an art workshop, because the weather was bad, etc., etc. The only time she didn't postpone was when she was sick. Don't ask me why.

"Are you really from America?" Ibrahim says, stopping his dribbling.

I nod. "From California. Where is your family from?"

"Algeria," Ibrahim says, in the same proud way I said "California." "Left when I was ten."

"Do you have a brother or a sister?" I feel like I can practice my French with a boy like Ibrahim, who is still working on his.

He laughs. "More than I need. Four little sisters and three little brothers." His eyes light up when he adds, "And an older brother. Moving here soon."

"You're lucky," I say. "I only have a little sister.

She's eight."

Ibrahim checks his watch. "Got to go." He sticks his soccer ball under his arm. "Can't be late for couscous night."

"What's that?'

"Dinner."

"It's early for dinner," I say. "It's not even four o'clock."

His eyes, the color of chocolate ice cream, darken. "No missing couscous night in my family. See you at school on Monday."

"See you at school on Monday," I repeat.

But when Ibrahim has turned the corner of the street and I'm sure he can't see me, I follow him. I've never been further than downtown and I'm curious to see what's beyond.

Ibrahim dribbles his way to the outskirts of town. Cars so dusty they probably don't run anymore are parked in weedy front yards. Four- and five-story gray buildings with narrow windows stand in the middle of parking lots. Laundry is drying at the windows, and exotic music and mouth-watering cooking smells waft outside. Couscous night sounds good to me. A teenage girl watches over kids bouncing and laughing on an old-fashioned seesaw. Older boys are playing soccer on a dusty patch of land. They greet Ibrahim in an unfamiliar language.

As he drops his soccer ball at the base of a bench, he glances mechanically toward the street. He spots me and his eyes lock mine for an endless second before he jogs toward me.

"Now," he says, pointing at me with his index finger. "Sit and watch."

I'm not so proud of myself for being a stalker, so I obey and watch him play. He's the best scorer of the team and the fastest on the field.

"Listen," Ibrahim says after the game, wiping off the sweat that drips from his brow with the hem of his shirt. "My life on this side of town stays here. Understood?" I nod. "Now," he adds. "Your turn. Take me to the other side."

5 LAC CHAGRIN

[*Sylvie:*]

Saturday is my favorite day of the week. School finishes at noon, and Maman makes steak and pommes frites for lunch. That's also the day I go to the library.

Mademoiselle Moulin waves from inside when she spots me parking my bike next to her rusty yellow Volkswagen Beetle.

"I've put something special aside for you," she says as she checks in the records I return. She leads me to her small office, where a pile of records crowds her desk. "I received new American music," she says. Her smile illuminates her warm brown eyes and ivory skin. "Something wrong?" she asks, when I haven't commented.

"I mean, right now, I'm more into French songs."

"Oh." She pushes away the records she had chosen for me. "I didn't know."

"Ok, I'll look at them," I say.

She spreads them out and slides one across the table. "Janis Joplin," she says. "Best white blues singer of all time. When I listen to her, I'm in America."

Now, that's the last place I wish to hear about, but I don't want to hurt Mademoiselle Moulin's feelings, so I thank her.

She sighs. "So much inspiration for young artists."

I like it when she talks about artists. My heart swells and I grow wings. In my wildest dreams, I fly above the low clouds that stretch like a blanket over Château Moines, and in a blink I'm in Paris.

Mademoiselle Moulin leafs through the pile of records. "I have many more, but I have to enter them in the catalogue first."

"I know someone who might be interested," I say, before remembering that I don't care about Scott.

"Really?" The prospect of a new library member brings color to Mademoiselle Moulin's pale cheeks.

"There is that boy in my class. Scott. He comes from California."

"An American?" She clasps her hands in delight. "Why didn't you bring him?"

I don't believe in fate or destiny or anything like that, but when the French doors of the library creak open on Scott Sweet *and* Ibrahim Maarouf, my lack of belief evaporates. A terrifying title flashes in front of my eyes: "Earthquake in Château Moines." Because if Ibrahim Maarouf, who has no friends in town and never sets foot in the library, is now hanging with

38

someone at the library, Scott Sweet is an earthquake in huaraches. The boys make their way inside and I shift my glance to the windows that open on the park.

"*Bonjour!*" Mademoiselle Moulin puts on her most cheerful voice and enthusiastic smile.

"*Bonjour,*" Scott says. If Mademoiselle Moulin wants me to listen to American music, Scott should listen to French songs to get the hang of our accent. "Can I look around?" he asks.

"Of course!" Mademoiselle Moulin says. "Sylvie told me about you. Welcome to Château Moines." But Scott has already disappeared behind a shelf.

Mademoiselle Moulin offers her warmest smile to Ibrahim. "Do you need help to pick some books?"

Ibrahim looks down at his pair of dusty boots. "Don't have a card," he says.

"You only need a proof of residence to get one," Mademoiselle Moulin says. "I have to remind your parents that they can stop by anytime."

"Got to go," Ibrahim says, and he is out before she can hand him an application.

She shakes her head and sighs. "Life can be overwhelming for recent immigrants. Hopefully when his older brother arrives, it will be easier for Ibrahim."

I'm surprised she knows about Ibrahim and his family, since he never comes to the library. I'm also surprised that she seems to care about them. Does she belong to this new association for immigrants that opened in town? Many people, my parents included, say that if we let the Arabs immigrate to France, there will be too many of them soon. I don't know what to think. Ibrahim keeps to himself. I like that, too. He loves soccer as much as I love writing songs. I'm not that different from him.

Scott emerges with a pile of books. "Where's Ibrahim?" he asks, looking around.

"He left," I say.

"Too bad." He settles his books on the desk. "Can I check them out?"

"First you need a card," Mademoiselle Moulin says.

"He can use mine," I blurt out, looking at the titles of the books he picked. Several classics of French literature are in his stack. I haven't read a third of them, and of those I read only excerpts anyway. I turn toward Scott. "You can check out your books on my card until you get your own." I catch a happy smile stretching Mademoiselle Moulin's red-painted lips.

"What did you say?" Scott asks in his funny French.

Mademoiselle Moulin repeats my offer and Scott nods. "*Merci*," he says. It sounds like *marsee*, coming out of his mouth. He narrows his eyes as if he were in deep thought. "You're friends with the girl who wants to help me with my French, right? The funny one? What's her name again?"

Why does he have to remind me of Annie? I slide my library card across the counter faster than I wish, and it falls to the ground. "Annie," I say between my teeth.

"And she's Sylvie," Mademoiselle Moulin says, picking up the card.

Scott's face breaks into one of his movie-star smiles. "*Merci*, Sylvie."

"While I check Scott's books out," Mademoiselle Moulin tells me. "Why don't you show him around?"

My card is one thing; a tour is another. But Scott doesn't give me a choice. He pushes the door that opens onto the graveled alley. "Are you coming?" he says.

Fresh air replaces the musty smell of the old stone walls and wooden floors of the library. Although I've decided to leave my hometown as soon as I have my high school diploma, I'll miss the library. It's housed in one of the towers of a medieval castle, shaded by ancient trees as tall as the smallest towers of the castle. I can hear the horses galloping and see the shimmering dresses of the ladies when I close my eyes.

"What's that?" Scott points to the lake that spreads like a luxurious emerald rug in front of us.

"It's Lac Chagrin," I say. "The legend says that a princess fell to the bottom and drowned. *Chagrin* means sorrow in French."

"I know what *chagrin* means," he says, his voice catching in his throat.

I glance at him and I have the feeling *chagrin* is more than a word to him.

6 BARE FEET FOR PEACE

[Scott, October 4, 1970]

The library books I borrowed last month crowd my windowsill. How could the librarian believe I would read all them in three weeks? I can't even pronounce the names of the authors. Only the name of Colette rang a bell, because Mom had some of her books at home, so I added Colette to my pile to show Sylvie I wasn't sexist. She didn't even notice. Instead of books, she checked out several French records. I didn't, because whatever plays on the radio and TV is so fast that I can only pick one word here and there.

It has been raining on and off since this morning. "Feelin' Groovy" is playing on my record player, but I don't feel groovy at all. The rain fills me with memories of stormy winter Sundays when Mom made French toast, and we'd eat it right from the pan, soaked in maple syrup and powdered sugar. Also Janis Joplin died today. Stinks.

Although I have nothing to do and I keep telling myself I should practice music again, I haven't touched my guitar yet. *Maybe my fingers won't know how to play anymore.* Plus I might not find any American sheet music here. After all, I haven't seen any music stores in town. "You're a chicken," says a small nagging voice in my head. Above my bed, Janis's smile seems to tell me, "Try just a little bit harder."

In a second, my room becomes a bottomless fishbowl, and I grab my jacket. I don't want to drown.

Dad is making a fire in the living room. Stacey is reading a French book out loud.

"Hey," I say. "I'm going for a walk."

Dad looks up at me, a log in his hands. "But it's raining."

"Drizzling."

"You already are a true Norman boy," he says with a smile.

"Can you bring me back one of those yummy chocolate croissants?" Stacey asks.

"In French, please," Dad says. "If you want one."

"Un pain au chocolat, s'il vous plaît?"

"Okay, then," Dad tells her. "You can have one."

Outside, the rain has stopped but the street is as empty as on a Super Bowl day. Where did everybody go? This morning, after church, they shopped like they had to be prepared for another Hundred Years' War against the British. Now only the bakery is open.

"Bonjour, Madame," I say to the woman who stands behind the counter.

43

"*Bonjour.*" Her voice and smile remind me of how great it is to have a mom. I search for the right words. "*Un pain au chocolat, s'il vous plaît, Madame.*"

She slides the pastry into a small bag. "Anything else?"

"*Non, merci, Madame.*" I'm getting the hang of the many polite expressions the French use for every occasion. I drop the exact change on the counter. I'm also getting good at recognizing the French francs and centimes.

The woman hands me the bag with a smile. "*Merci et au revoir.*"

"*Au revoir, Madame.*"

A girl bounds out from the back of the store and gets behind the counter. "*Salut,*" she says.

"*Salut,*" I repeat. An amused smile curves her lips. What's her name again? "You're Sylvie's friend," I say. "You work here?"

Her smile fades. "I *live* here. And by the way, you're lucky we're open for cleanup. Everything's closed on Sunday in France."

The woman who helped me looks kindly at the girl. "Annie, why don't you show this young man around? He's new and—"

Annie! That's what Sylvie called her. Annie rolls her eyes. "He's from San Francisco," she says.

"Santa Monica," I say.

She ignores me and adds, "He knows what a town is."

"Not a town like ours," the woman says.

She has a point. Even the traffic lights are different here than at home. Besides, nobody cares about them, and crossing rue Principale is more dangerous than crossing Pacific Coast Highway 1.

"Your mother's right," I tell Annie.

"She's not my mother!" Annie hurries out of the shop.

"I'm Annie's foster mother," explains the baker, and she retreats to the back of the store before I get a chance to say *au revoir*.

I spot Annie perched on one of the benches that line rue Principale. I pass her without a glance.

"Have you been to the forest yet?" she asks and before I answer, she has jumped down from the bench. "This way," she says, jerking her thumb down the street.

I should probably go home, since I have Stacey's snack. She'll be mad at me if I'm late. But Annie is leading me toward the public park, and I'm getting curious. With the rain and wind most trees have lost their leaves. Back home, the palm trees make a mess when they shed, but here my flip-flops go deep through a thick mat of brown leaves that stick to my feet. I should consider switching to my Birkenstocks. Annie struggles to walk in her platform boots. We walk through the gates, which open on the park, and I follow her to a fence.

"There is another set of gates, but this is a shortcut." Annie squeezes her body underneath. As I bend over, she warns me, "Careful. It's an electric fence."

We stand next to each other on the other side. Annie turns toward me. "Let me show you the forest and its creatures from the beginning of time." I chuckle, and she brings her index finger to my mouth.

"Hush," she murmurs. Her skin is soft and smells of warm bread. "It really is an old forest." She steps away. "Come on."

Since we walk in silence, I have plenty of time to think of what she just did. Why did she touch my lips? It must mean she likes me. Am I supposed to do something? Do I like her?

We go on through the forest and I observe the trees. Their gnarled limbs remind me of old people's bodies. Small trails branch out from the main one. The forest must be even deeper than it looks. In the shadiest areas, the smell of wet wood and mushrooms is as stinky as rot.

Once in a while Annie peeks over her shoulder to check on me. I don't dare ask her where we're going. As long as I stick with her, I assume I won't get lost. Besides, we're staying on the same trail. The shaded path widens to an alley, and we reach a small meadow, bordered with large rocks. Tables and benches have been placed here for a picnic area. The bench Annie picks is damp, so we sit on top of the back.

"Tired?" she asks, elbowing me.

I shake my head *no*, focusing my attention on my muddy feet.

"You should put real shoes and socks on." She jumps down and picks up a stick to remove the mud from her boots.

"I won't wear socks until the war is over," I say.

Her eyebrows shoot up. "War? What war?"

"The Vietnam War." I scrape my feet against my jeans.

"Forget about the war," she says, stretching her arms wide open. "Look how beautiful it is around us. I like to come here." She leans closer to me. "You can come with me. I told you I could help you with your French."

I'm not exactly sure of the deal here, and I keep my mouth shut and my eyes on my feet. The good thing about not being fluent in a foreign language is that it gives you an excuse to remain silent. Another good thing is that Pete and Mike are in California. They would laugh so hard if they saw me being so lame with a French girl.

"It sure is a big forest," I say when I find the silence too heavy.

"Huge." Annie zips up her tight green vinyl jacket. "Don't ever go beyond this meadow or you could get lost." She looks at me straight in the eyes. "Nobody comes here. If you came with me, it would just be the two of us."

I tighten my grip around the pastry bag. "Are you hungry?"

"Starving."

I split the pain au chocolat in two and give her the

largest half. Every girl in every country must appreciate this act of generosity. I'll deal with Stacey later. Annie licks the chocolate from her fingers while I search my brain for the right words to ask her out, but I can't find them.

Besides, Sylvie's face crowds my mind for no reason, like the clouds, white as popcorn, that are now filling the sky.

7 DRAWBRIDGE TO PEACE

Since Scott arrived, words and notes shot out of my pen. Ratatatatat. They don't make beautiful sentences, even less a song.

Week after week,
Day after day,
It's a fight for Scott.
School's a battlefield
To win the love
Of the beach boy in exile.

In class, I rack my brain, hoping to find a` clever topic of conversation, but I have been mute most of the time, until I bump into him at noon on Saturday.

"Huh," I start, pulling on my sweater sleeves. "Want to go to the library this afternoon?"

Scott's a head taller than me, since he is perched on his roller skates. "I didn't finish my books," he says, as he eats the heel of a fresh baguette.

It's a relief when I remember the pile he borrowed, and I realize he's not just avoiding me, but it's a disappointment too that he doesn't need to go to the library. "Meet me there at two o'clock," I say in a daring move. "I want to show you something."

"Okay," he says, and he slaloms away between pedestrians, who curse him.

I check my outfit in the mirror in La Boutique. Not too bad, if I skip the homemade jeans and focus on my sailor striped T-shirt. It's not an Indian tunic, but it's my best-looking shirt. I brush my hair and leave it down. On my way to the library, I'm agonizing about what I can show Scott. Nothing in Château Moines can impress a boy from California. Mademoiselle Moulin is stepping out of her VW Bug when I park my bike. She smiles mechanically when she sees me.

"Have you heard?" Her voice cracks a little. "Janis Joplin is dead." She flops onto the stone bench right outside the library. "It's ridiculous to feel sad for someone I never met, isn't it?" she says.

"I don't know," I say with a shrug. Mademoiselle Moulin remains silent, and I'm relieved to see Scott showing up on his roller skates.

"Janis Joplin died last week," he says. "Not even a month after Jimi Hendrix."

"It's sad," Mademoiselle Moulin says, and she retreats inside the library.

"At least," Scott says, "they leave us their records so we can enjoy their music forever." He takes his skates off. "Some people die, and it's just over."

I have no opinion on the subject, since I've never lost anyone close to me. Only Mémé's husband is dead, but he passed away before I was born.

Scott pulls on the fringes of the scarf wrapped around his neck. "Ibrahim gave it to me. Do you want one too?" he says when he catches my glance. "This scarf symbolizes the fight of the Palestinians for freedom."

If Maman thinks that Levi's and army bags aren't feminine, I don't feel like asking her opinion about pro-Palestinian scarves. "I don't know," I say with a shrug.

"I think that world peace starts with promoting it around us," Scott says, trading his skates for a pair of strange-looking sandals.

"Uh," I say. "Hey? Want to see a drawbridge?"

"A real one?" Scott widens his eyes as if I was flying him to the moon.

"Of course, a real one!" I say. "I told you I had something to show you."

Scott follows me as I take him to the drawbridge. "Where does it go?"

"You see the manor?" I say, pointing to the other side of the bridge.

"Can we go inside?"

"It's closed to the public."

"Too bad," Scott says. He looks down at the drawbridge. "It's cool. Was it used often?" he asks, observing the thick wood and heavy chains of the bridge.

"What do you think?" I say. "Of course it was. Château Moines had to protect itself against invaders. Remember that France is a land of many wars."

"We are at war too," Scott says.

"We?"

"America is at war in Vietnam."

"Of course," I say. I'm not exactly sure of what's going on in Vietnam, but I know it was a French colony and it's not anymore.

"As we speak," Scott says, stopping halfway across the bridge, "American soldiers are getting killed because Nixon doesn't want to end the war." He pronounces the name of the American president the way Mémé says the name of Pompidou, the French president, because he's from the Right and Mémé votes Socialist.

Now I remember: When the French left Vietnam, chaos swarmed over the country. And that's when the Americans arrived to try to defeat Communism.

"War is wrong, wrong, and wrong," Scott says, hammering in his words with the heel of his weird sandal.

"Careful," I say. "This bridge has seen many battles, but the wood is rotten."

Scott grabs my arm. "This bridge carries the blood and the suffering of people," he says. "That's why it's important to oppose war and promote peace."

I shake my arm free. "Is it why you have so many peace signs on your jacket?"

"You've noticed?" He models his army jacket, embellished with peace signs and names of places I've never heard of. "I've been to dozens of sit-ins and peace rallies. I know everything about protests."

"Me too!" I blurt out.

Scott waits for me to elaborate.

"We've had tons of protests in France," I say. "Have you heard of May '68?"

"My mother told me it started with the students' revolution in the Latin Quarter." A veil passes over his face. "So, how was it?"

"We occupied the universities," I say. "We fought against the police, we burnt cars and we built barricades." I'm on a roll, and I add, "A true social revolution," making a mental note to remember that title for a future song.

"Cool," Scott says in English.

"Huh?"

"*Chouette?* Is that what you say in French when something is cool?" When I nod yes, he adds, "I'll definitely seek your help to promote peace awareness around here."

I would definitely ruin everything if I told Scott I was only ten years old in May 1968 and that the only things I did was race my bike like a maniac, watch TV because school was closed, and go fishing with my father because he was on strike.

So I smile a confident smile and say, "Groovy!" in my best American accent.

8 HOLLYWOOD FOLLIES

[*Scott:*]

"Voilà!" Dad flicks the lights on.

I blink and shade my eyes with my hand. Around me, crates of all sizes fill what looks more like a warehouse than the store under our apartment. I read "Los Angeles" on the labels and "LE PETIT PARIS" on a rusty neon sign stuck in a corner.

"What's going on in here?" I ask, glaring at Dad.

He sits cross-legged on top of a wooden crate. "I told you I had plans," he says with an amused smile.

"*This* is your plan?" I don't know how many boxes are in here, and I don't even know when and how they came, but I have no doubt that Dad isn't himself anymore. Stacey and I agreed that going to France was a good idea; now I'm not so sure.

My sister snakes her way between the crates, some of them so tall that she disappears behind them. "What's inside?" she asks. "Can you open one?"

"Absolutely!" Dad jumps down. He pries open one of the crates. Then he gets a cutter from his back pocket and slices the top of a box open.

Stacey peeks inside. "Clothes!" She squeals with delight, digging through the box. She pulls out several pairs of jeans. "What are these for?" She raised her eyebrows, waiting for an explanation. Dad smiles mysteriously, which gets on my nerves but brings a grin to Stacey's face.

"The boutique!" She throws her arms in the air. "You're opening the boutique!"

The whole place resonates with their exclamations and laughter. In a way it feels good, but I know the idea of a store came from Mom, so in another way it feels like we are stealing her dream and cheating her.

"Mom wanted a store," I tell Dad when he emerges from behind a box.

He brushes his dusty jeans and looks me in the eye. "That was what she wanted most," he says.

Yeah, in Santa Monica, not in a small French town, I think. Roughly estimating the number of boxes, I figure that Dad must have spent thousands of bucks to order whatever else is inside. It's a little worrying, but my father hasn't been looking forward to anything for six months, so I high-five him.

Stacey runs all over the store, chirping like an excited bird. "Oh, Daddy! This is so groovy! Every girl in my class will shop here."

When I remember the clothes some of my classmates wear, I suppose there is the potential for business. Expectation makes Dad's eyes shine, so I say, "When are you opening?"

He scratches his chin. "The sooner, the better." He shifts his eyes from one corner of the store to another. "We have an advantage." He points to the old sign. "Le Petit Paris was a clothing store before. The shelves, the racks, and a lot of stuff are still here."

"I'll help!" Stacey says, putting her hands on her hips.

"That's my girl!"

"First," she says. "We have to find a name."

Dad pulls out a piece of paper that was stuck in his back pocket. The paper is so creased I think it will crumble into dust. "Your mom found the name."

Stacey's sticky hand slips into mine. I pretend to pinch her and she does the same, but I feel her pulse beating against my palm, and it squeezes my heart. Stacey needs a mom, and she only has a brother who doesn't feel that groovy and a father who chases dreams as if they could glue together the pieces of his broken life.

"Ready?" Dad's voice catches in his throat. He unfolds a piece of paper so thin and faded that I know he has kept it in his pocket since Mom wrote the name on it. "Hollywood Follies," he reads. He blinks his eyes. "It's good, isn't it?"

"I love it!" Stacey hugs Dad, and I wipe my clammy hand on my jeans.

Dad smiles at me and I smile back. Stacey makes a

pirouette between the crates. Dad rolls his eyes, pretending she is the silliest girl on earth, and I do the same.

The next few days melt together, until I am not sure what the date is. We wake up, have breakfast, Dad works at the store while Stacey and I are in school, we come back, do our homework, help him, have dinner, work some more, and fall asleep on the couch, which would never ever have happened with Mom. My dreams each night are filled with cans of paint and brushes, with hammers and buckets of nails.

We have a week off from school and we take full advantage of it. By the end of the fall break, the previous owners wouldn't recognize their store. I don't recognize us either. Dad hasn't shaved, and dark stubble covers his cheeks and chin. Stacey can't get rid of the paint that's stuck under her fingernails, and my hands have grown calluses. We haven't eaten anything but sandwiches made of baguettes, ham, and cheese.

On Sunday night, Dad makes a pasta dish. A well-deserved treat. "We did it!" he declares, twisting off the top of a bottle of Perrier. "*Santé!*" he says.

"To Hollywood Follies!" Stacey says, bringing her glass to Dad's and then to mine.

"To Hollywood Follies!" Dad and I shout back.

Dad puts the Doors on the record player, and we sip our Perrier, accompanied by Jim Morrison, and take our first real look at the store since the previous week.

Each wall is painted a different color, since Dad has divided the store into world areas. Africa is brown and yellow, Asia is pink and gold, Europe is green and silver, and America is red, white, and blue. He has painted the world's flags, and I have handwritten PEACE in as many languages as I could. In each section, racks of clothes and native crafts represent the style of the different continents, and even countries.

"It's really far out, Daddy!" Stacey says, running her hands along the clothes that swing on the racks.

"Careful!" I snatch her hand away. "We want to sell them too!"

She rolls her eyes. "Mom would love this place," she says in a soft voice, and I throw my arm around her shoulders.

We go to bed late, but earlier than we have all week. Dad plans to open on Tuesday morning, since most businesses are closed on Monday in France. That night I dream that Mom is visiting the store. I wake up before knowing if she likes it or not.

"There's something you've got to see," Dad says at breakfast. He leads us outside on the sidewalk.

"Whoa!" Stacey cranes her neck to admire the awning that shades the store. "You made it?"

"I ordered it," Dad says. "What do you think?"

"Cool!" Stacey says.

A sun, a moon, and zillions of stars are splashed on the dark purple background. The word PEACE, translated into several languages, imitates the Hollywood Boulevard Walk of Fame and matches the inside decor. There are also peace signs painted in the center of the sun and moon. I recognize the name Mom chose when I read "Hollywood Follies," but I see Dad's spelling when I catch the two L's in "follies."

"*Folies* has only one L in French," I say.

"Your mom wrote it that way," Dad says.

"This is the English spelling." I doubt Mom would have made a mistake.

"She wrote it that way," Dad insists. "I couldn't change it. Come on, you have to get ready for school."

I go back inside, wondering why Mom, who was fluent in French, would have misspelled a word on purpose. She always said Americans were suckers for French names. With the correct spelling, I suppose. Maybe she thought French people were suckers for American names also.

9 FOLLIES WITH TWO LS

For the last three years, I've stopped by the bakery to pick up Annie on my way to school. I just love the early morning smells of warm bread and pastries that float through the bakery.

The bell rings when I push the door open. Elle trails in, right behind me.

"*Bonjour, petites.*" Monsieur Duval, Annie's foster father, bakes all night; his white hat is a little crooked in the morning, and traces of flour line his face.

On the other hand, Madame Duval, with her fresh coat of lipstick and ironed dress, looks as perfect as the croissants she displays in the window.

"Annie is almost ready," she announces with a warm smile.

"I am," Annie says, emerging from the backroom with her satchel.

"Did you eat your breakfast?" Madame Duval

asks.

Annie rolls her eyes and waves a paper bag.

"Did you drink your chocolate milk?" Monsieur Duval says.

Annie shrugs.

"You'll be hungry," Madame and Monsieur Duval say with a sigh heavy with worry.

I don't know if Annie hears them wishing her a good day before the doorbell rings behind us, or if she notices that they wave at us until we are out of sight.

Holding her croissant between her teeth, Annie digs into her satchel. She hands my sister a couple of pink meringues.

Elle pops both in her mouth. "*Merci*," she says. My sister would do anything for meringues.

"Have you checked the list of books we've got to read before the end of the year?" Annie asks me.

"It's November. Are you helping Scott yet?"

"Either he's totally deaf or stupid, because he ignores me when I ask," she says between mouthfuls. "Good luck to him if he trusts Brigitte," she adds with a smirk. "It's not like she has ever aced any French test."

Annie is now attacking a brioche she must have slipped into her pocket.

A flow of words rushes to my mind.

Invisible war
Rages at school.
Boy in favor of peace

Turns eventless school
Into a combat zone
And quiet lives
Upside down.
Is it what peace is about?

Elle smacks her sugarcoated lips. "Everybody should help Scott," she says.

"Thanks for the advice," Annie says, with a nod in Elle's direction. "I'm afraid it won't work."

"Because you all like him?" Elle says.

I wonder how Elle and I can be related. There is nothing that I like more than turning off the racket around me and writing down all the words and music that flood into my head. Elle, on the other hand, asks questions, makes up her mind, and gives her opinion.

Annie flaps her hand at Elle. "Boys are way beyond your worries, little girl."

"I'm not that little," Elle says. "Besides, we have exactly the same issue with his sister." She looks up, her big eyes shaded by her straight bangs.

Annie stops munching on her brioche. "What do you mean?"

"Stacey is in my class."

"Who?" Annie asks.

"Stacey Sweet," Elle says with an exasperated sigh. "Scott's sister."

"You didn't tell us he had a sister," I say.

"Like I had a chance. It's Scott this and Scott that. For your information, he has a sister and she teaches us English," Elle goes on. "And we teach her French.

We all take turns." She pauses and asks Annie. "Do you have a timer?"

"Do you also give her French cooking lessons?" Annie asks.

"Our teacher sometimes has to use a timer when it's the boys' turn." Elle lowers her voice. "They *all* like Stacey. Especially petit Paul."

"*We* might need a timer, then," I say.

Annie shoots me a dark glance and I shut up. We walk to the elementary school in silence until we drop Elle at the gate.

"Easy for you to joke about sharing Scott with a timer," Annie says, making a funny face. "You don't even like boys."

"I like boys," I say. *It's not because I don't want to like Scott that I don't like him.*

Annie tilts her head and grins. "Really?"

"It's not like there are many boys here, anyway."

"What?" Annie slaps her thigh. "There are plenty. Look!" She points across the street to a bunch of boys entering the elementary school.

"They are Elle's age!" I exclaim, recognizing petit Paul from Elle's class.

"More on the way!" Annie is on a roll.

"That's Ibrahim!" He shepherds his sisters and brothers, who crowd around him.

"So? He's a boy. Look! More here!" Two other boys from our class are coming our way. "And there!" Annie goes on, but she stops in her tracks.

Scott is stepping out of a store I've always seen

closed. Instinctively, Annie and I have slowed down. We are both taking in his unusual yet already familiar silhouette, and I catch Annie unzipping her vinyl jacket. Underneath she wears a skintight sweater. She flips her hair with a twist of her head. I've no doubt that, like me, she finds Scott irresistible.

But unlike me, who freezes when he turns his head toward us, Annie waves her hand. "*Salut*, Scott!" she calls.

He waves his hand back. *"Bonjour!"*

I pick up my pace, but Annie reaches Scott before me. She grabs him and pulls him against her chest.

"Hey," he says.

"Isn't it the way Americans say hello to their friends?" Annie says, triumphantly.

"It's called a hug," Scott says, pushing her away.

If I could be like Annie! I would show Scott our French way to say *bonjour* and would kiss him on the cheeks.

"What's that?" Annie asks, pointing to the most extravagant awning I've ever seen in Château Moines.

"My dad's store," Scott says. "Come on, we'll be late." He starts off, but Annie claws at his arm.

"Wait a second." She narrows her eyes. "Sylvie? How do you spell '*folies*'?"

I peek at the awning. "F-O-L-L-I-E-S," I spell out loud. "American spelling, that's all."

Annie eyes me with suspicion, but Scott's smile beams out like one of the yellow suns above our heads.

Although I didn't crush him against me, I'm on a cloud.

10   A GHOST TOWN

[*Scott:*]

Last night, Mike and Pete called me from California.

"I can't talk long," Mike says. "International calls, you know. How's it going?"

"Fine," I say, observing how the evening sun draws cool shadows on the walls. "And you?"

"Groovy."

"The French say *chouette*," I explain to Mike.

He tries to repeat and it makes him laugh. Then Pete gets on the line.

"Baseball without you is kind of boring," he says. "Hey, you know what? The Sunny Shake made a new drink in your honor. They call it 'The Parisian.'"

"I don't live in Paris, you know."

"No difference," Pete says. He lowers his voice. "Hey, how are the chicks?"

I don't have the heart to tell him that my love life is nonexistent or to ask him about his own, because I feel as if we're on the same remote island in this chapter of our lives, so I say, "Chicks are the same all over the world."

"I agree on that one," Pete says with a sigh.

I know he's trying hard to pretend there are not 6,000 miles between us, so I don't tell him how messed up I feel most of the time. "How's your brother?" I ask instead.

"He's missing basketball like crazy, and he hates taking his medicine. So he's pretty crabby."

There is a long silence while I easily picture Jake, so athletic before his injury, and now stuck in a wheelchair. Don't tell me we should wait patiently for the end of the war.

In an exaggerated cheerful voice Pete says, "What about the music?"

"I haven't found a music store yet."

"That's bad, Dude! You know what? I'll send you some records from home."

"That would be groovy, thanks."

"I've got to go," Pete says. "Cool talking with you."

"Same here. Bye."

I hang up, thinking that the saddest thing is that I don't really miss Pete, Mike, or my school. I don't even miss the baseball games or the music store. We were so miserable in Santa Monica that Stacey and I agreed with Dad that a change of scenery would be better. Yet I can't help thinking there is more to the move, so I hate Mom for being dead and Dad for hiding something from me. And I hate myself for thinking that way.

I'm now in French class. Through the window I follow the useless fight of the leaves against the wind. They spin in the air, wingless paper planes, before crashing on the wet pavement. I feel as helpless as they are.

Monsieur Leroy snaps his fingers, and I land on planet school. "Next Monday," he says, "we'll have the annual school medical visit."

I squirm on my bench. "Medical visit" in French sounds close enough to English to tighten my stomach. Can't foreigners be excused?

"We?" Annie says. "Are you going to get weighed and checked too, Monsieur?"

"Annie, since you show so much eagerness to participate, would you mind reminding us what we have to bring to the medical visit?"

Annie looks down at her open notebook. "I forget."

Everybody remains silent, and I suspect there is some kind of major embarrassment.

"Bring a urine sample in a small container," Monsieur Leroy says as he writes it as an assignment on the board.

What? Pee in a cup and bring it to school? The French are really weird. Where can I find a booklet listing my immigration rights? There must be something.

68

"With a lid on the container?" Annie asks. The whole class bursts into laughter, giving my poor stomach a break.

"Yes," Monsieur Leroy says with a nod. "With a lid. And your name on top of it."

"Oh, that I wouldn't have forgotten," Annie responds. "I wouldn't want my sample to be mixed up with anyone else."

"*Dégoûtant*" Brigitte pouts, and waves her hands in the air. Her bracelets bang around her wrist. "Don't you think it's *dégoûtant*, Scott?" she asks me, batting eyelashes heavy with mascara.

Although I know that *dégoûtant* means disgusting, I know that taking one side or another can only make things worse. No need to start another battle between the girls, so I conveniently shrug.

"Bodily functions," Monsieur Leroy says, "are only disgusting when people keep talking about them. Urine and blood tests are a good way to check our general health."

"Still, Annie can be so disgusting," Brigitte says.

"Case closed," Monsieur Leroy says. "Oh, I forgot: no homework for tomorrow."

Everyone shouts, "*Ouais! Merci, Monsieur!*"

"You're welcome. Now, let's open our Latin books."

The recess bell rings at that second. Monsieur Leroy flips the blackboard to the clean side while everybody dashes out.

Annie and Sylvie take a seat on the low wall next

to our room. Brigitte drops down next to them, and Annie squeezes closer to Sylvie. She pats the wall for me to sit down. The only spot left is between her and Brigitte, so I skip the offer.

"I hate the medical visit," Brigitte says.

"Me, too," Sylvie adds, in her usual quiet voice.

Annie leans forward, and her breath smells of the bubble gum she popped in her mouth. "Last year, we had to stand in our underwear for more than an hour."

"Don't believe her," Brigitte tells me. "She exaggerates."

Sylvie doesn't comment, but her cheeks redden.

"I'm hungry," I say, hoping to change the subject.

Brigitte splits her cookie and offers me one half. "Chocolate," she says.

"Here!" Annie hands me a perfectly round cookie. Brigitte shoots her an evil eye.

"*Merci*," I say, embarrassed when I spot Sylvie's cookie divided in two equal parts. She closes her hand onto them, and her green eyes look away.

"Say, Scott," Annie asks, licking the crumbs from her lips. "Are you going to catechism on Thursdays?"

"Catechism?"

"That's what I said." Annie narrows her eyes. "Or do you belong to another religion?"

"We're not sure where we'll worship." I don't feel any obligation to tell the whole world that I've pushed God to the darkest corner of my mind. "I saw two churches in town," I say when I feel Annie observing me, waiting for an answer.

Brigitte giggles. "It's not like you really have a choice. Both are Catholic." She tilts her head. "I go to Saint Pierre's," she says in a voice as sweet as her cookie.

"That's also mine," Annie says. "I always sit in the third row."

"Which one is your church?" I ask Sylvie, who hasn't said anything.

"My family goes to Saint Jean's because mass is at eleven and not at nine like at Saint Pierre."

I laugh. "It's a good reason. I'll have to remember that."

"Hey, Scott," Annie says. "What exactly is your family doing here?"

"Excessive curiosity can be a sin," Brigitte says, before I come up with an answer.

Annie puts her hands up, which I take for an apology. "People wonder why you came here, that's all," she says.

"Because," I say. "Santa Monica had become a ghost town."

Brigitte gasps, Annie widens her eyes, and Sylvie lowers hers.

11   LEVI'S 501 AND A MYSTERIOUS GIRL

[Sylvie, November 12, 1970:]

Florence just paid me for her wedding dress," Maman says, as we turn onto rue Principale. "I'd like to buy fabric and make you a pair of nice pants and a blouse."

"Can I buy a pair of Levi's instead?" I ask.

"I'll probably even have enough for—"

"Maman! I said a pair of Levi's."

"And what on earth is a pair of Levi's?" The way she pronounces my favorite brand name would be funny if we hadn't been at each other's throats since this morning because of them. "And remind me already," she says. "Why are they so special?"

"They are American jeans. And everybody but me wears them."

Maman's pointy heels beat the sidewalk with vengeance. "I can make you clothes you won't find in any store," she says between lips glazed with a fresh coat of lipstick.

"I know you are very good, it's just that…"

Maman shoots me a look, and we go on without exchanging a single word. We could walk rue Principale blindfolded. The boutiques never change, the owners only get older, and their children take over. But we are now approaching Hollywood Follies, and my mother can't pretend she does not see the purple awning with the name printed across it as if someone had handwritten the letters. Yet she doesn't slow down, although she tightens her grip on the straps of her handbag.

I catch up with her. "Why don't we peek inside this new boutique?" I say, as if I had given up on the Levi's. "It looks *chouette*."

My mother stops a few feet away from Hollywood Follies. "If I had a store that big," she says, without really talking to me, "I would offer much more than my wedding dresses. I would carry hats, gloves, purses, and every accessory for a wedding. Even shoes." She snaps her fingers. "Everything would sell as fast as the baker's baguettes."

"I've always seen this place closed," I say.

"There was a clothing store here before," she says, ignoring the funky window. "It was called Le Petit Paris."

"I had no idea."

"The owners died in a car accident, and their only daughter didn't want to deal with the store." My mother stands immobile on the sidewalk.

"Why?" I ask.

Her voice strangles in her throat when she says, "I don't want to talk about it."

"What happened?"

"Nothing."

If it's nothing, why does my mother seem upset? It's only a store after all. Her surprising reaction is on my mind as she picks up her pace. It looks like she has pushed the store out of her mind, but I see how she takes in the colorful awning with a glance full of disdain.

"A business owner who doesn't know how to spell," she says, "doesn't deserve my patronage." She peeks in the window, using it as a mirror to fluff her hair, while I take in the T-shirts and the tunics displayed on a thick layer of sand and the jeans hung on palm trees and cactuses. Flags of many countries billow out under a huge fan. I am dying to go in, but Maman speeds up and I follow her.

We've just passed the store when someone calls my name. Scott is seated cross-legged in front of the entrance to the apartment next door. He isn't even wearing his Indian sandals, and his bare feet are tanned like mine are in the summer. Smells of exotic musk and incense drift into my nose, and I feel an irresistible sneeze tickling my nostrils.

"Bless you," he says.

"*Merci*," I say, sneezing once more.

"Blow your nose," Maman says.

I snatch the handkerchief she hands me and stuff it in my pocket just in time, before Scott bounces to his feet.

"*Enchanté, Madame*," he says, extending his hand, which my mother has to shake. "*Je m'appelle Scott.*" Despite my embarrassment, I melt under his polite tone of voice and his delicious accent, but my mother only nods as she grabs my sleeve and pulls me away.

"*Au revoir,*" Scott says.

I feel so humiliated that I don't have the guts to say "*Au revoir.*"

Maman lets go of my arm when we are at a safe distance from Scott. "What kind of mother would let a boy walk barefoot?" she says, but again she isn't really talking to me. I don't feel like telling her that I doubt there is a mother at Scott's house.

The covered market smells of fresh mushrooms and grilled chestnuts. Most vendors bribe us with slices of fruit or cubes of cheese, but Maman ignores them and chooses a corner booth.

"The usual," she asks the vendor. "Plus a kilo of red grapes." She doesn't glance at the chubby cabbages or the sandy leeks. Our garden produces all the vegetables we need. While she pays, I put the fruit in our canvas bag.

"We need eggs and butter," Maman says, checking her list. "Milk, cheese, and *crème fraîche.*" She elbows her way to the dairy booth and I tag along.

The chickens send desperate piercing SOSs across the market each time one of them is packed away. Women greet my mother and ask her how she's doing. Maman is all nods and smiles. As she is being served at the cheese stand, I shift the bag from one hand to another to balance the weight. Accidentally, I bump into someone waiting in line behind me. I peek over my shoulder and recognize our next-door neighbor.

"*Pardon, Colonel*," I say. "*Comment allez-vous?*"

His military medals bounce on his chest as he taps the ground with his cane. "How am I supposed to be well when the Général has just died?" he says.

I have no idea who he is talking about, and I'm glad Maman jumps into the conversation. "France lost a hero," she says, lowering her eyes.

The Colonel nods. His mouth tightens in pain when he limps away.

"Général de Gaulle led the French Resistance during World War II," Maman tells me. "It may not mean a lot to you and other young people, but for the Colonel, who went to war, and even for me, the Général symbolizes the fight against the German Occupation."

Scott would like the guy. I should ask him if there is someone like him in Vietnam, a general who opposes the Occupation of Vietnam by the American army.

The bag I carry is bursting at the seams. It smacks against my legs as I try to keep up with Maman, imagining how life was for her when she was a kid in an occupied country. It's hard to imagine, and I wonder why Scott cares about a war kilometers away from here.

"Sylvie!"

This is Elle's voice, and my blood swooshes through my body. On our way to the market, we dropped her off at Mémé's, but I don't see my grandmother.

Maman rushes to my sister's side. "Where is Mémé?"

A fluffy mass of blue hair pops up right behind Elle. "I hate to be cooped in on market day," Mémé says. "How are you, *ma belle?*" she asks me with a playful smile.

"Come on," Elle says. She drags the three of us to the clothing section of the market. "I want you to meet my new friend."

Stacks of T-shirts and tunics, silky scarves, and exotic jewelry cover every centimeter of a table. A rack displays different styles of jeans. A vendor I've never seen before stands behind the table, and a little girl in a pair of roller skates is waving a sign, WELCOME TO HOLLYWOOD FOLLIES! WORLDWIDE STYLES BROUGHT TO YOUR DOOR!

Both man and girl are tanned and smiling. The little girl wears her sun-kissed hair down, but the man's is in a loose ponytail. They wear similar faded bell-bottom jeans and Indian tunics.

"This is Stacey!" Elle points to the girl. "And her papa. She calls him Daddy."

My mother has no choice but to shake the man's extended hand. "I'm Doug," he says. I let out a sigh of relief. At least he hasn't hugged her the American way.

"Madame Pottier," Maman says, retrieving her hand. "And my mother and my daughter Sylvie," she adds.

Doug smiles and then straightens a pile of T-shirts on the table. "I figured the market would be a great way of showing what Hollywood Follies carries," he says.

My mother looks away, but Mémé responds with a seductive smile, "Doug, I wish I could speak English like you speak French. If I may ask, where did you learn?"

Scott's father bows. The necklaces he wears cling-clang. "*Merci, Madame,*" he says. "I spent some time in Paris years ago. That's where I met my wife, a French native," he adds, and the same veil I've seen passing over Scott's eyes goes over Doug's. He rearranges the jeans on the rack.

"Here, Daddy," Stacey says, handing him a pair.

Mémé taps my shoulder. "I like the clothes," she whispers. And with a mischievous nudge she adds, "And the man too."

"Mémé!" I say with a giggle.

Today my grandmother wears a pair of yellow pants and a matching blouse. Her dyed hair compliments her blue eye shadow. Mémé is the only one who forgets that she has lived through the First and Second World Wars. As for men, my grandmother carries my grandfather's handkerchief in her pocket, sprayed with his cologne.

Maman clears her throat. "And how long are you

staying?"

"Forever," Stacey pipes up. "We live here, right, Daddy?"

"Absolutely, darling." The way he says "darling" makes me wish for Papa to be home. "We are here for good," he adds, meeting my mother's inquisitive stare.

I suppose Santa Monica has become a ghost town for good if they moved here.

Mémé throws her arms wide open. "Then," she says. "Welcome to Château Moines and long live Hollywood Follies."

Without a word, Maman turns on her heels, heading to the opposite side of the market. My grandmother tightens her hold on her macramé bag.

12 LA CLEF DE SOL

[*Scott:*]

Days blend into each other and I can't tell them apart. When I'm finished with my homework, I find myself with so much free time that I wonder if France has more than 24 hours in a day. French kids don't have school on Thursday. That's when they play sports and go to catechism. Since I don't play soccer and they don't play baseball, I don't play a sport. Since I gave God the silent treatment after Mom died, I decided to skip catechism. The result is that Thursdays feel longer than any other day.

Pete kept his promise and has sent me the latest album from the band Chicago. Jake has drawn a peace sign and a happy face on the cover. I keep playing "25 or 6 to 4" over and over again, thinking of him and wondering how he can still believe in the peace sign after what happened to him.

Other than the medical visit that wasn't so bad

after all, although carrying a container full of urine was gross, nothing is happening and, again today, I wander through the sparse apartment. I wonder who is sitting on the furniture we sold at the garage sale before we left. It gives me the blues to think about it. Maybe going to town will change my mood.

Stacey is seated cross-legged on the rug, using the coffee table as a desk. She's twirling a strand of her hair as she concentrates on her math homework. I want to go to town, but I know she'll want to come.

"Hey, Stacey," I say. She looks up from her book. "I need to go to town. Dad told me he just received a shipment from L.A. Clothes, jewelry, perfumes, you know, that kind of stuff. Do you want to come with me or help him unpack?"

In a blink, Stacey folds her notebook and slides her arms into her sweater. "I'll stay with Daddy," she says. I smile, satisfied with myself.

"I'll be back soon," I tell Dad. "Anything you need from town?"

"Bread and cheese," he says. "You know the cheese we bought the other day? Creamy but not runny?"

"Right," I say, although I have no idea what he's talking about. The dairy shop has so many cheeses that it must take the French a lifetime to learn half of the names.

Today rue Principale feels like the Santa Monica boardwalk. Although it's November, the sun makes everything bright and cheerful, and people chatter and laugh while they shop. If only some of them would stop by Hollywood Follies! Business is slow at the store. Dad explained that it's because of the high unemployment rate in France. But nobody is naked, so I figure they must spend their money elsewhere.

Deep in my thoughts, I haven't noticed a man walking toward me, and I bump into him. I'm so surprised that I excuse myself in English.

"*Pardon?*" he says in French, and in a glance I take in the collection of war medals displayed on his jacket. This is the man they called the Colonel at the café the day I bought a Coke. Staring at me with the exact same suspicion in his eyes as he had that day, he hammers on the sidewalk with a well-crafted cane.

"*Pardonnez-moi,*" I say.

"*Pfft,*" he says, which I take for "apologies accepted." He taps my shoulder with the tip of his cane. "Be careful next time, *jeune homme.*"

I don't know what goes through me, but the way he calls me "young man" and taps me with a cane doesn't seem right. "Violence is not the answer," I say.

The Colonel stiffens, and his face reddens. He straightens his grip around the knob of his cane. "And who are you to lecture me?"

"Monsieur," I say. "I don't believe that using your cane as a weapon is good."

"First of all, call me Colonel. Second of all, I earned my cane." He brandishes it in the air, and as he shifts his weight, I realize with horror that he only has one leg.

"I'm sorry, Colonel," I say, thinking that whenever and wherever there is war, the results are the same. Jake in Vietnam. The Colonel in France. The same terrible mess.

"Don't ever feel sorry for me," the Colonel says, shooing me away with his cane.

I hurry down the street, mortified and angry with the Colonel and with myself. People crowd the terrace of Chez Lili, and I spot Garçon, carrying a load of drinks on a tray. I slow down to cross the street, but he has seen me.

"*Salut, l'américain*," he says. "A soda or a Coca-Cola today?" His mocking laugh follows me, and I pick up my pace.

I stamp down the sidewalk with rage, until I find myself in a part of town I haven't seen yet. I look around and spot what I need.

A music store is squeezed between a bookstore and a grocery store. Spider plants, hung in macramé nets, swing above a black-and-white sign that reads "*La Clef de Sol.*" My entrance jolts a man who is dozing behind the counter.

He takes off his glasses, wipes them with the hem of his denim shirt, and sighs. "A natural vibrato," he says to himself, and I understand he's talking about Joan Baez, who can be heard singing in the background.

The man pushes a stained cup and half a sandwich aside to reach for his pack of cigarettes. He lights a match and finally sees me. "Bonjour," he says. His voice sounds like he has a sore throat. "Can I help you?"

"I'd like some sheet music for guitar. Rock and ballads."

"Then you came to the right place." The man scratches his dark beard, grabs an elastic band, and ties his long hair in a ponytail. He puts his glasses back on and his glazed eyes light up. "Follow me." He bounces down from his stool.

With his pair of frayed jeans, smiley face button pinned on his shirt pocket, and his long hair, he reminds me of Santa Monica and, despite everything, I find myself smiling. *I've just met someone Dad might like.*

The man takes me to the far end of his cluttered shop, humming to the music. Along the way, I take in the walls covered with concert posters, record covers, odd job offers, and community announcements. Most are in French, but I catch a few posters of the Rolling Stones, the Beatles, and Chicago as well. We reach a smaller section of the store, with bins filled with alphabetically organized sheet music.

The man turns toward me and extends one hairy hand. "They call me Troubadour," he says.

"My name's Scott." I shake his hand. "My dad opened Hollywood Follies."

"Great name," he says with a warm smile. "I wish I had thought of it."

"*La Clef de Sol* isn't bad either—the Treble Clef?" I ask.

A phone rings somewhere. Troubadour leans against one of the bins. "Do you need more help, or can I leave you?"

"I'll be fine, *merci*."

He makes a small salute and goes to the phone. Before he returns, I find what I am looking for.

"If you play every day," Troubadour says, slipping *The Best of Simon and Garfunkel* into a paper bag, "you'll have mastered these by Christmas. Then you can move on to a more advanced level."

I pay him and tuck the bag under my arm. "Thanks for your help."

"Listen," Troubadour says. "Every year, I throw two concerts. Consider yourself invited to the Christmas concert. You could perhaps play in the spring one."

"Really?" The perspective of playing for real is both exciting and scary. It'd be so much fun to play with other people, but what if I haven't learned anything by spring?

"I said 'perhaps,'" Troubadour says. "Now, go home. You have some work to do. I do, too." He starts tuning a guitar. As I close the door, he makes the same little salute with his fingers.

For the first time since we arrived, something is stirring inside me. I don't exactly know what to call this feeling, but finding a music store and meeting Troubadour is like drinking a cool glass of water after playing baseball in the summer.

13 PAPA IS HOME

[*Sylvie:*]

Elle takes off when she spots Papa's truck parked off the street. I'm also impatient to see him, so I hurry after my sister. Papa's semi is so long that the trailer blocks part of the Colonel's driveway.

In fact the Colonel is in his yard, and as soon as I'm within earshot, he calls, "Tell your father he can leave his ..." he points to the semi, "whatever the name is, he can park it here until tomorrow morning."

I know how much Papa hates to have to park his truck at Transport Européen for the night when he has been on the road for weeks. "Thanks," I say. "He'll appreciate it."

"*Pftt*," the Colonel says, and he limps back to his house.

Fresh coffee and warm pound cake aromas waft into my nose when I push our front door. Papa's really home! I find him, Maman, and Elle around the kitchen table. Chocolat leaves my father's side and nudges me with his wet nose.

"*Ma puce!*" Papa stands up and opens his big arms. I snuggle in his embrace, but why do I have to think of Scott? I would hate it if he found out that my father calls me his flea. "I missed you," Papa says, kissing both of my cheeks.

His stubble scratches my skin. A blend of gasoline and fried food smell rises from Papa. The odors will fade after Maman has washed all of his clothes, and will only vanish when he starts driving the Peugeot instead of his truck. It's like having two fathers.

"I missed you too, Papa," I say. "*Comment ça va?*"

"Much better, now that I'm home," he says, sitting back in his chair. Chocolat curls up at his feet. Maman slices the cake, slides the largest piece onto Papa's plate, and pours some steaming coffee in his cup. "Best coffee in the world," Papa declares as he puts his cup down. He takes a big bite of pound cake. "Best cake in the world."

Maman blushes, Elle claps her hands, and I look away.

"So, girls, how is school?" Papa asks. "Anything new?"

"Oh! Yes!" Elle says through a mouthful.

"Empty your mouth while Sylvie tells me everything."

"Not fair." Elle wipes her mouth with the napkin Maman hands her.

"Not much to tell you," I say. "Nothing new really."

"Not true!" Elle says. "We've got kids from America! Stacey is in my class and she is my bestest friend."

"Best," Maman says, and I catch Papa's smile.

"Anyway she's *chouette* and she has a brother in Sylvie's class. His name's—"

"Maybe Sylvie wants to tell your father about him," Maman says.

"Thanks, but no thanks," I say, stabbing my slice of cake with my fork.

"My secretive girl!" Papa says with a laugh. "Well, I'm glad school seems to be fine. Enjoy being kids! Worries come soon enough, believe me." He stands up and digs through his large duffel bag. "Ah! Here they are!" He pulls out four plastic bags and divides them into two sets.

My sister squeals with delight as she finds a shirt with little ducks printed in the center, some jewelry, and a little purse inside her bags. With a quick glance I see that the inside of my bags the things are exactly the same, only in a bigger size.

"Sorry, but I have some homework to do," I say, dropping the bags on the table.

"Can I have your slice of cake?" Elle asks.

"Help yourself to my gifts, too," I say, catching my father's pained look.

I push my chair back. Chocolat shoots me a worried eye. I climb the stairs two at a time, my dog at my heels. I shove the door of my room open. Chocolat settles on my bed, as I pull my trunk from underneath. I flip my notebook open to a blank page, but I have the feeling I will write hateful words, so I lock it away. My dog follows each of my moves with his teary eyes.

I can't stand staying in the house that closes in on me, so I put my pea coat on and throw the records I borrowed from the library in a bag. Papa and Elle are still in the kitchen. The humming of Maman's sewing machine covers the sound of my feet as I tiptoe to the door. Chocolat sticks to my heels, but I nudge him away.

I bike up to the library. The crisp air calms me, and I regret having left home without telling my parents. Without parking my bike, I drop my records in the return box at the back of the castle. As I pedal to the main path, I catch sight of someone leaning over the railing of the bridge.

"Careful!" I shout, pedaling as fast as I can. In a few seconds, I've reached the bridge.

"Sylvie! Is that you?"

Why of all people does it have to be Scott? He's wearing a colorful knitted hat with flaps that cover his ears. Ridiculous. "What are you doing here?" he says.

What is that supposed to mean? Isn't it my home here? I turn my bike away.

"Wait!" he calls. "I'm all right, you know," he says, walking toward me. The gravel crunches under his sandals. "Thanks for reminding me that the water is

89

deep and the wood rotten."

He brings his hands on my handlebars. His blue eyes have darkened, as if the night has changed their color. "Hey, would you like to go for a walk in the forest with me?" He's watching me toy with my brakes. "Tomorrow, two o'clock?"

"Okay," I say. He lets go of my bike.

It's only when I reach home that I realize with a jolt that for the last three years, Saturday afternoons have belonged to Annie and me.

14 A *CABANE* IN THE WOODS

[*Scott:*]

"This is a very ancient forest," Sylvie tells me, as we step onto the winding path I took with Annie back in September. She glances at me. "*Ancient* means very old."

I don't feel like telling her that ancient is also an English word. I can't believe she's here with me. Yesterday, when I offered to take a walk with her, I was 100% sure she had already some plans and would say no. When she agreed, I thought she wouldn't show up. But here she is, with her long hair that falls past her shoulders, and her green eyes that remind me of the waves crashing on the beach back home. She has brought her dog Chocolat, a dark brown Labrador. Chocolat walks ahead of us, wagging his tail, while his nose grazes the path, following a trail invisible to us. Like the first time I came here, there is something in these old trees that makes me believe they are spying on us before closing in right behind us. I would hate to get lost here.

Sylvie's carrying a basket, and when she notices my glance, she opens it to show me a baguette, a chunk of cheese, and two canteens. I also spot a couple of dog biscuits and, at the bottom, some blank paper and a few pencils.

"In case we get hungry," she says.

"Cool," I say in a detached tone, although it's weird and exciting that a French girl has packed a lunch for me.

"The forest," Sylvie explains, "has always been the town kids' playground. My parents and even Mémé played there."

"Mémé?"

"My grandmother. My mother's mother. I call my father's parents *Grand-père* and *Grand-mère*. They live far away, so I don't see them as often as Mémé. What do you call your grandparents?"

"I never knew my mom's parents," I say. "They lived in France but died a long time ago. My dad's parents live in Seattle. I call them Nana and Papa."

"*Nana* is a *chouette* name for a grandmother," Sylvie says. "*Papa* is for fathers in France." She points at the trees. "I used to build tree houses when I was little. Then Annie moved here. She prefers hanging out in town, so I haven't been here for a while."

"I've been here once before," I say.

Sylvie slows down and turns toward me. The green of her eyes matches the leaves of the old trees. "It is beautiful around here. And hardly anyone comes here."

I fall silent as I remember Annie telling me the same thing a couple of months ago. Chocolat barks at the crows hovering above us. My Birkenstocks crunch through the thick mat of leaves and sink into the moss. I've no idea how long we've been walking, but we've passed the meadow I discovered with Annie. We aren't even on a trail anymore. Weeds taller than Chocolat scratch my feet. Annie warned me to stay on the path or I could get lost. We've hiked for another ten minutes or so when something catches my attention.

"Hey! Look!"

"What is it?" Sylvie asks, looking in the direction I'm pointing.

A small building can be seen behind a thick grove. I push some crooked branches aside, and we inch our way toward the structure, partly hidden by the trees. The sound of flowing water accompanies us. There must be a river close by. Tree by tree, the woods thin, and soon we reach a clearing. A shed made of wood sits against a hedge of oak trees.

"I've never seen it before," Sylvie says.

"You said you haven't explored the forest in years."

"I don't think I ever walked this far anyway," she admits.

Two dusty windows face us, and a few steps lead to a plain front door. A crooked chimney sticks up from the roof. Empty clay pots are half buried underneath a rotting bench. Chocolat shifts his gaze from Sylvie to me with wonder and excitement in his eyes. He sniffs the ground, wags his tail, and nudges Sylvie, begging for a decision.

I climb the narrow stairs, which squeak and wobble under my sandals. Chocolat is on my heels and shoves me with his wet nose when I turn the doorknob. It's locked. The dog cocks his head, looking as disappointed as I feel.

"Come on," Sylvie says. "We should go."

I turn the knob a little bit harder. Still the door doesn't budge. Thick spider webs cover the window. I wipe them off with my sleeve and peek inside.

"Don't see much," I say, scrubbing a little harder.

"I'm leaving," Sylvie announces.

"Don't be a chicken," I blurt out in English.

She frowns at me. "What did you call me?"

"It's just an expression."

She shoots me a dark eye. "For your information, in French we say, 'Don't be a wet hen.' I'm neither a chicken nor a wet hen, but I really think we should go."

"Hah! Come on!" She doesn't move an inch. Chocolat shifts his glance, unable to take sides. "It's not a crime to look through a window." I step aside so she can get a glimpse.

Chocolat stretches up and leans his paws against the windowsill. I elbow Sylvie. "See the rusty rake and the shovel? This shed's abandoned."

"Are you sure?" She twists her hands around the handle of her basket.

"Positive."

"It doesn't mean it's ours." She steps away from the window.

"Private property is overrated," I say. "You know what?"

"Yes?" she says with a sigh.

"This shed can be our secret place."

"What?" She widens her eyes in disbelief.

"Like a club." Excitement grows inside me. I've built countless castles on the beach, but never a tree house. And I've never found an abandoned shed in a forest. "What do you say?"

"We can't." Sylvie drops to the ground. Chocolat lies down at her feet, his head on her lap.

"Why not?"

She scratches her dog between his ears. "I already told you—it's not ours."

I sit down next to them. "Look, we are actually giving this place a second chance." I pick out the leaves stuck between my bare toes. "Like my dad with the store."

"What if the owner comes?" Sylvie says. Chocolat opens a lazy eye.

"We'll tell him we had no idea it belonged to someone." The dog closes his eye. "We could bring a couple of chairs, a table, some pillows, and food," I go on. "This place is perfect for working on the peace rally."

Sylvie folds her arms around her legs. Chocolat slips to the ground, heaving a loud sigh. Only the sound of the stream running in the distance reaches us.

"We can't even get inside," she says. "There isn't a key."

I jump to my feet and overturn the crumbly clay pots, one by one. "Ah! I knew it," I say, brandishing a rusty key.

The door unlocks after a couple of tries. Sylvie follows me inside. Spiders have made themselves at home, and a thick layer of dry leaves coats the rough floor. Dust flies up as we walk across the shed. Sylvie sneezes and steps outside.

"It has some potential," she says. She studies the shed with her slanted eyes. "Champignon!" she exclaims.

"What?"

"A clubhouse needs a name. See the branch above the roof?" She points at the sky. "It makes like a big umbrella above the shed. Looks like a mushroom, doesn't it? *Champignon* means 'mushroom.'"

"Hmm. Let's see." I'd prefer a name like 'Woodstock' or 'Genesis.' Or 'Apollo.'

"It's really just a *cabane*," Sylvie goes on. "You know what a *cabane* is, right?"

"Of course," I say. "It's a cabin, in English."

"This is it, then," she says. "*La cabane*."

I nod, relieved that she picked a name easy to pronounce and not some kind of weird French name, such as Champignon.

Sylvie rummages in her basket and gets a piece of paper and a pencil. "A club needs rules," she says, handing me the pencil.

I put my hands up. "You write. French spelling is too tricky."

"Okay, but you tell me what to write." Sylvie wets the lead of the pencil.

I take a deep breath and dictate in my best French: "La Cabane belongs to members Sylvie Pottier and Scott Sweet."

Sylvie's eyebrows shoot up, but she doesn't say anything. So I go on: "Sylvie Pottier and Scott Sweet are the founding members of la cabane, making them permanent members. Nobody can become a member of la cabane without the accord of both founding members."

Sylvie recopies the rules onto another piece of paper and hands me one.

"*A notre amitié*," she says. Her voice is a breeze on my skin.

"To our friendship," I say in English.

Chocolat wags his tail in agreement.

I jam the paper in the tight front pocket of my jeans. As I move, Mom's turquoise earring tumbles out and lands on the grass.

"Oh!" Sylvie exclaims. She picks it up. "It's beautiful," she whispers, as she slips the earring into my palm. Like Annie's, her skin is warm and soft against mine.

I tuck the earring into my pocket. Sylvie cocks her head as if she expects me to give her an explanation, and Chocolat does the same. But all of a sudden, his nose sniffs the air, his ears point to the sky, and he takes off.

"Chocolat!" Sylvie shouts her dog's name and whistles.

Only the rustling of branches and the crunching of leaves answer her call.

15 ELLE IS ON THE LOOKOUT

[*Sylvie:*]

"Where did he go?" Scott has stopped and is catching his breath. "Has he ever done that before?"

I shake my head *no*. Like him, I'm out of breath. "Bizarre. Chocolat would only take off after someone he knows."

"We haven't seen anyone." Scott peeks at his watch. "Geez, it's late, I've got to go. Will Chocolat find his way back?"

"I bet he's already on his way, while we worry for nothing," I say, but I'm worried.

We walk home, keeping our eyes peeled for a dog, but we reach rue Principale without finding him.

"Got to go," Scott says, still looking at his watch. "Good luck, and keep me posted."

I rush home, hoping all the way to spot my dog, but no such luck. The house is quiet when I come in.

The door of La Boutique is ajar. A gown as white and light as a summer cloud is spread on the couch, and Maman's chair is pushed aside.

Elle appears from nowhere. "Maman ran next door," she says, "to bring some vegetables to the Colonel." She lowers her voice. "And Papa is napping."

I'm relieved that I don't have to face my parents right away.

"Where's Chocolat?" Elle says, looking around. "Didn't you take him with you? Where did you go? What happened?"

As I'm searching for a smart answer, the doorbell rings. "I'll get it!" I shout, glad to escape the questions Elle is firing at me.

Annie stands at the door. "I think you lost someone."

My dog bounces around me, licking my hands. I pet his thick brown coat and, in a sudden surge of love for him, bury my nose in his fur.

"Thank you so much! Where did you find him?"

Annie narrows her eyes. "Look," she says. "I don't care if you ditch me for the new boy in town. But you could have called. I waited all afternoon for you."

"I'm sorry. Thank you for Chocolat."

"Thank you for being my friend," Annie says in a hissing voice. She turns her heels, climbing down the steps.

"Hey," I say, on a sudden impulse. Annie tries hard to be tough, but I didn't miss the hurt in her voice. "Would you like to be in a club?"

Annie wheels around. Her eyes register surprise. "I hate clubs. They're like families with rules everybody has to follow except the ones who make them. Why are you asking?"

"It doesn't matter," I say, feeling an immediate rush of relief and shame.

Annie shrugs and walks away without a single glance in my direction.

I close the door and climb up to my room. I slump onto my bed and get my notebook. The only thing on my mind, now that Chocolat is back and Annie doesn't know anything about la cabane, is the earring Scott keeps in his pocket. A melody and the new lines of a song burst to my mind.

The sun kissed the turquoise
Pure as a sky after the rain
Raw as sorrow and loneliness
Yet warm as a heart and a promise.
The precious stone flickered
Like a star watching from above.

Chocolat's scratching at the door, followed by Elle's quick footsteps, jolt me. In panic I reach for my trunk and drop my notebook inside. I push the wooden box back under my bed and flop onto my chair as my sister enters the room. I prop my math book open in front of me. Chocolat hurries to my side and rolls onto his back.

"What were you doing in the forest?" Elle asks. Suspicion thickens her voice.

I feel her inquisitive glare on my back. "Huh?" I say, rubbing Chocolat's belly, soft as baby chicken's down. My dog moans in delight.

Elle sits at her desk. "What did you do in the forest?"

"Scott and I took a walk," I say as if it were no big deal. "With Chocolat." Hearing his name, my dog leaps to his paws.

"And Chocolat got lost?" Elle swivels on her chair.

"He just didn't want to be cooped up again; right, Chocolat?" He pants, drools, and sighs in agreement. "He got sidetracked, that's all."

Elle twirls a strand of hair between her fingers. "Stacey just called. She said Scott wasn't home either. Do you know where he is?"

Too bad my notebook is away, because words jump at me.

My sister's on the watch.
Always watching me,
Like a cop on duty
My sister's watching me.

"No idea," I say. "Anyway, I'm glad Annie found Chocolat." My dog looks up at me, and I tickle the top of his head.

"Annie was weird when she returned him." Elle touches the tip of her nose. "Something's fishy."

"Don't be a *flic*," I say through my teeth.

"I'm not a cop, I'm just observing."

"Come on, Chocolat," I say, pushing my chair back. "Let's get out of here."

Downstairs, Maman is preparing dinner and Papa is reading his newspaper. We haven't spoken much since he returned home with his gifts for eight-year-old girls and told me I should enjoy being a kid. I'd like to avoid him, but he looks up from his newspaper when he hears me. His face breaks into a grin.

"*Ma puce*, could you go get me the newspaper?"

Maman fetches money from the money jar. "We also need bread," she says.

Papa slips one franc into my hand. "Buy yourself a treat."

I squeeze the coin in my palm. "*Merci.*"

"If you get candies," Maman says, wiping her hands on the dish towel, "keep them for after dinner. Also, the dog stays inside." Chocolat whines, but I'm out before he and Maman complain more.

A line snakes its way through the bakery. Annie stands behind the counter, and our eyes meet. At that second, questions fire my mind. Was she in the forest? Did she see la cabane? Did she see the earring?

"One baguette, please," I say in a thin voice.

Annie hands me the bread as if she were blind or I was invisible. I drop the bill on the counter, waiting for the change. Her icy glare hits me like a sheet of rain.

I hurry to Chez Lili, where I buy Papa's newspaper Ouest France and a pack of gum for me. I'm unwrapping a stick when I spot Scott sitting at a window booth. I don't want to talk to him and I rush to the door, but he has seen me.

"Wait!" He runs after me. "Is Chocolat okay?" he asks when he has caught up with me. He wraps his hand around my wrist.

The calluses at the tip of his fingers scrape my skin. "Annie brought him home," I say, sticking my gum in the hollow of my cheek.

"That's great, then," he says as if now everything was fine. "Did she find him in the forest?"

"She didn't tell. Did she tell you?"

Scott frowns. "You look like you are angry at me."

"Why would I be angry at you?" I ask with a shrug. He lets go of my wrist. "Should I be angry at you?"

"La cabane," he says. "Monday after school."

I still feel the warmth of his hand through my sweatshirt, seconds after he leaves, but I shiver.

Scott hasn't answered any of my questions.

16   FIRST CUSTOMER

[*Scott:*]

I don't get it! Sylvie was so worried about her dog when we lost him; she should be happy that Annie found him. Why is she angry with me? I hope she's in a better mood when we meet at la cabane Monday after school.

I grab my guitar and flip open my music book to the last section. Troubadour was right; I'll have learned all the songs by Christmas. I have to tell Dad about the music store and Troubadour. I'm pretty sure the two of them will hit it off. But I haven't seen my father much these last days. I wonder what keeps him busy, since the store is quiet most of the time. The ringing phone startles me.

"Sweet residence, good afternoon," my sister says, in perfect French. "Of course, no problem." She hands me the phone. "It's for you."

"*Allo?*" I say.

"This is Mademoiselle Moulin, the librarian."

I remember with a start that I haven't touched a single book I borrowed back in September. "I'll return my books tomorrow."

"*Non, non,*" she says. "I knew you would need more than the regular three weeks. I'll make sure Sylvie doesn't have to pay any late fees. I just want to tell you that the library is open late on Saturdays. Between school and your father's busy schedule, I figure that you'd like to know about more options for coming to get your own card."

"Thanks," I say, toying with the phone cord.

"Voilà," Mademoiselle Moulin says.

"Voilà," I say. She laughs a kind small laugh. "I mean '*Au revoir,*'" I say.

"*Au revoir.* For the card, I told your father I need a proof of residence, such as a phone or utility bill. Could you remind him?"

"Is there a problem?" Stacey asks when I hang up. She looks at me. Worry fills her eyes.

Back home, for more than a year, most of our phone calls meant bad news. I shake my head and say on a cheerful tone, "No problem at all. Everything's great."

Stacey returns to her homework. The muffled noise of the cars that stop and go along rue Principale doesn't slow down my thoughts. I had no idea my father knew the librarian, much less that he knew her well enough that she has our phone number.

"Do you mind if I play my guitar?" I ask my sister.

She gives me one of her big smiles, reminding me

so much of Mom. "Play the Bee Gees!"

They have never been my favorite band. "I couldn't find the Bee Gees," I say. "But I have 'I Am a Rock' by Simon and Garfunkel."

Stacey jumps to the sofa, curling up with the pillows. As soon as I pinch the strings, she sings at the top of her lungs, covering my mistakes. We end up yelling the words like two lunatics, and we are attacking another song when Dad comes in. Right away he joins us, and the three of us scream like there is no tomorrow. When our throats are so scratchy that we can't sing another word, we drop onto the sofa and laugh until Stacey has to run to the bathroom.

Dad rubs his teary eyes, and I'm not sure if he's laughing or crying. "It's so good to let go of everything. Thanks, son." I just nod. He points at my guitar. "I'm proud of you, you know that?"

I nod again. His words make me feel good, but they embarrass me too, so I'm glad to see Stacey.

"I'm hungry!" she shouts. "I want pasta."

I'm sure Dad is grateful, since he doesn't know to cook anything but pasta. He puts music on and he cranks the stereo volume up so we can hear it from the kitchen.

"Stacey, get the largest pot," he says.

I fill it with water, and Dad throws in a few pinches of salt. Stacey gets the spaghetti from the pantry. Dad opens a can of tomato sauce, and I grate some Parmesan.

"An Italian feast!" Dad says.

I crave Mom's steak au poivre and homemade potato puree more than ever, but I say, "Nothing is better than pasta, anyway."

Dad pats my shoulder. "I've some news." Stacey gets closer to Dad. "Good, of course!" he says and Stacey smiles. "I sold two pairs of jeans and three T-shirts yesterday afternoon!"

"Yeah!" Stacey high-fives Dad. "Way to go, Daddy!"

"And to the same customer!" Dad checks the water in the pot. "A cool lady who also bought some incense and a bunch of candles."

"That's really good news, Dad," I say. *If business booms, maybe I can work at the store and with the money take some guitar lessons.*

"Did you have any other customers?" Stacey asks, handing Dad a wooden spoon.

"A few people came in and browsed, but nobody bought anything."

"Not yet!" I say. "But they'll be back, I'm sure."

Dad nods and smiles at me. "Thanks, son. By the way, you two know my new customer. She's the librarian."

"Mademoiselle Moulin!" Stacey says. "You know what? She just called."

"Really?" Dad says, checking the water once more. "Almost boiling. Did she want to talk to me?"

"No." I throw the whole packet of spaghetti in the pot. Hot water splashes over the counter, but neither

Dad nor Stacey notice. They go on chatting together as my mind churns with bothersome questions.

Why would the librarian want to talk to my father? It's not like they know each other. Dad said she's a new customer. But then she has our phone number.

Then, I decide, looking sideways at my father, *I won't tell you about Troubadour tonight.*

17 THE TURQUOISE PENDANT

[*Sylvie, November 23, 1970:*]

The dismissal bell rings, and Annie makes a mad dash to the door. All around me people are making plans for the rest of the afternoon, but I remain seated, unable to decide if I should go to la cabane or not.

Scott rushes outside, his bag slung across his chest. An unpleasant feeling hits me. Is he ditching me for Annie? Did he forget he invited me this afternoon? I wish I could take off after both of them and pretend there is no problem. But I can't keep faking. It has been another bad day. Since she brought Chocolat back home, Annie is not the same. First I believed she had seen Scott and me, but she looked clueless when I mentioned a club. Now I think it's just because of Scott, and I hate it that he takes so much space in my head.

When Brigitte sees me behind my desk, she walks

over. "Is something wrong between you and Annie?"

I shrug one shoulder; I have no intention of confiding in Brigitte.

"Are you sure?" She brings one hand to her hip and the other to her hair. She catches my glance at her wide-legged jeans and her tight turtleneck. "I just visited my brother in Paris," She tilts her head. "It's the only place to shop, really."

I'm glad Brigitte forgot her initial question. But she leans closer to me. "Of all people, you know that Annie has excuses. She's craving attention, that's all. I forgive her for her bad mood and you should do the same."

I don't know yet if "The Socialite Is a Shrink" would make a good title for a song, but I should give it a try.

"Nice talking with you," I say, taking off.

Brigitte flaps her hand at me. "Anytime," she says.

I dash to the elementary school, thinking of what Brigitte just said. How could I have forgotten that before she moved to Château Moines Annie had never stayed for more than a year with the same foster family? I suppose she must be happy the Duvals have kept her for that long. But maybe she worries that they will want to get rid of her. That would explain a lot. But not her being cold with me. I'm deep in my thoughts when I get to Elle's school.

My sister is waiting with Scott's sister. "You are late," they both say in English.

"Hello to you, too," I say. They clamp their hands

over their mouths to cover their giggles. I turn to my sister. "We've got to go, Elle."

"Can you walk me home?" Stacey asks, lacing her roller skates. "My brother is busy this afternoon."

My heart drops as I realize that Scott has really ditched me. "I'm not sure," I say.

"It's okay," Stacey says. "Sorry for asking."

Her balance is wobbly on her skates, and she trips. I catch her before she falls and get a glimpse of a pendant dangling under her tunic. I'd swear that the turquoise color is identical to the earring Scott keeps in his pocket.

Stacey holds onto my arm. "Thanks."

"All right, I'm taking you home," I say. "But hurry up, both of you. I also have things to do."

Elle elbows Stacey. I steal a look at her as she whispers, "Told you!"

I grab her hand and Stacey's, and we cross the street. We leave Stacey under the awning of Hollywood Follies.

"Thank you for walking me home," she says. Her smile lights up her small face. "It was nice of you."

"You speak French even better than Scott," I say.

She mimics a curtsy, and once more I spot the turquoise pendant. Elle catches my eye and looks at Stacey's shirt.

"Oh, that is a pretty necklace," she says.

Stacey lowers her eyes. "It was my mom's," she says. Her voice is soft, but her fingers squeeze around the jewel. She stuffs it underneath her tunic. When she looks up, her eyes and voice are cheerful again. "Why don't you come in for a minute?"

Elle tags along and I follow them inside Hollywood Follies. The mix of musk and patchouli oil flies me away from Château Moines. My eyes can't take in all the clothes and accessories, crafts, and decorations that fill the store.

A pang of understanding for my mother hits me. In a real store like Hollywood Follies, my mother would have mannequins with different faces and hair to display her beautiful gowns. Customers would pick their fabric from among meters of muslin, organdy, silk, linen, and tulle, which would be stored on shelves. Catalogues would be arranged on low tables, and comfortable armchairs would welcome the brides-to-be. Compared to Hollywood Follies, La Boutique is a shack.

Footsteps break the flow of my thoughts when Stacey's father bounds from the back of the store. He kisses the top of her head. A knot rises to my throat, as it reminds me of how I have grown distant from my father.

"*Bonjour*," he says, extending his hand. "Sylvie, right?"

I shake his firm hand. "Yes, I am Sylvie," I say, rattling for a few words in English. It makes his blue eyes twinkle with kindness.

"Thanks for walking Stacey home. Scott said he's working on his French with a classmate this afternoon. The quizzes and tests freak him out."

I can't imagine Scott freaking out, but I must accept that he either lied to me or to his father.

"We have to go. Nice meeting you. Good-bye." I pull my sister to the door.

"Not so fast." Elle shakes her arm free.

"Told you, I'm busy this afternoon."

"What are you doing?" she asks. I ignore her, and she slips her hand in mine.

We walk home in silence, my thoughts focused on Scott's earring and Stacey's pendant. So identical, they can only go together. As soon as we arrive, I rush upstairs and open my trunk.

The beginning of a song quivers in my mind and I begin to write:

What is your secret?
Hidden beneath glimmer and glamour
Lies a bed of
Sorrow and tears.
Enigma surrounds you,
Heavy and solitary.
What is your secret?

Stacey said the pendant was her mom's. Scott said Santa Monica had become a ghost town. I'm sure that their mother once wore the turquoise pendant and a matching pair of earrings. She doesn't anymore. Did she divorce her husband? Did she leave them? Or did she die? How can you ask a friend such questions? Maybe you don't if you are a friend. Maybe you just go on being the best friend you can be.

I tuck my notebook away, but on a sudden

impulse I stick it in my back pocket. I'm not sure Scott will be at la cabane or who will be with him, but I've just made up my mind. I'm going.

"Maman! I'm going to Annie's. We've a school project."

Maman appears with a pair of scissors in one hand and a box of pins in the other. She got a big order for a winter wedding and her eyes are red from lack of sleep. "Bring back some bread then," she says.

I don't want to see Annie, but I agree.

It is past 5 o'clock when I park my bike behind the library, next to Mademoiselle Moulin's empty parking spot. The sky is the color of a blackboard and the sun is a piece of chalk that draws strokes of red and orange on the horizon.

I hurry along the graveled alley and quicken my pace along the trail. Darkness and silence fall like a cloak on me, and my heart marches up and down my chest. I sprint on the last section of the path, and I'm out of breath when I reach la cabane.

Scott is sitting on a picnic chair outside, holding a flashlight above a book. The leaves that crunch beneath my shoes give me away. A grin breaks his face, and he jumps to his feet. A South American poncho is draped on top of his army jacket, and his ridiculous hat with flaps covers his ears, but he still doesn't wear any socks.

"I thought you forgot," he says. "Come on, I've something to show you." He waves his flashlight toward la cabane, cranks the door open, and closes it behind us.

18 NO BARRIERS FOR MUSIC

[Scott:]

I switch my flashlight off.

"What are you doing?" Sylvie backs up and grabs the doorknob.

I switch my light on, and she takes in the candles I've lit on top of the folding table I brought.

"What is it all about?" Her hand tightens on the knob.

"I told you I had something to show you." I hand her my flashlight.

She looks around and spots my guitar. "Is that yours?" Her hand relaxes around the doorknob.

"That's what I want to show you," I say, grabbing my guitar. "Sit down."

She hesitates, but switches the flashlight off. The candles flicker and Sylvie sits on the edge of one of the pillows. I plop down next to her. She moves a few inches away from me, hiding her face behind her long hair.

"I used to play the guitar," I say. "I've decided to give it another chance. So I'm kind of rusty, if you see what I mean." The beginning of a smile stretches her mouth. *Yes! She likes music!*

I've practiced before she arrived, but when I play "Let It Be" I'm so nervous that my fingers slip and miss a string. Sylvie's eyes glow under the flames of the candles. Her smile is so encouraging that, song after song, I relax.

"Sing with me?" I ask.

"In English?" She sounds panicked.

"It's not like my French is perfect. Mom always …" Saying "Mom" aloud crowds my heart with too many memories. I jump to my feet so they stop haunting me.

"If you want to talk about your maman …" Sylvie says in a soft voice.

I flip open my music book and turn the pages as fast as I can. I'm upset that Sylvie guessed something about Mom, since I haven't told anyone. At the same time, a strange relief washes over me. I keep the book open and strum my guitar.

"I'll sing with you," Sylvie says.

Her voice is very soft and reminds me of the French singers Mom used to play back home. It should make me sad, but for a weird reason I feel better.

"I thought you didn't sing," I say. She smiles, but doesn't say anything. "I can't feel my fingers anymore." I rub my calluses against my jeans.

"I also have something for you," Sylvie says. Her voice is so quiet that I think I've dreamed it, but she gets up and pulls a notebook from her back pocket.

She leafs through it and picks a page filled with tight handwriting. Her hair falls across her face and the smell of lemon transports me home. Mom always picked a lemon from the backyard that she squeezed, and she added the juice to our shampoos.

"You play the guitar," Sylvie says. "I write songs." Her green eyes look straight into mine. "I've never showed them to anyone. In fact, nobody knows that I write songs." Her hand shakes as she flattens the page. "Can you read my music and accompany me?"

I'd like to tell her that I was scared to death when I played earlier, but I keep my mouth shut and instead get my guitar. I'm amazed that Sylvie can bring so many nuances to her voice. Thanks to Mom, I understand enough of the French words to get the general meaning and I can concentrate on the notes.

As I listen to Sylvie, the coolest thing happens. I stop paying attention to every word and instead focus on the music they make. No more barriers of language. Outside, an owl hoots and the stream whispers. The night is a warm coat that smells of leaves and wood. I wish words and music could hover above us forever. When we are finished, we don't talk at all, but it's okay. The silence feels as snug as the poncho on my shoulders.

"I've got to go," Sylvie finally says, avoiding my

eyes.

"Your songs are very good, you know," I say. "I could accompany you with my guitar. We could play together at the spring concert at La Clef de Sol." She remains silent. "I mean, if you want."

She stands up. "I need to get bread for dinner."

"Me, too."

I would have found any excuse to stay with her for a little while.

19 SILENT TREATMENT

Scott and I walk back to town in silence, but for the first time since Annie stopped talking to me and I started to avoid Papa, I feel light and comfortable. It's as if our sharing of music and lyrics has been a long conversation between Scott and me, and we don't want any words to spoil it.

The night wraps us in a cool and eerie coat, but since we are together I'm neither cold nor afraid. Our breaths coil into the air, and I wonder where they meet and where they vanish together. The lights of town flicker in the distance and, though they feel familiar, I also dread going back to the real world.

Maybe Scott feels the same way, since he says, "We could go to Chez Lili and listen to music."

"That's would be *chouette*, but I have to get bread," I say. "My parents will throw a fit if we don't have any for dinner."

He smiles one of his beautiful smiles. "Bread is

sacred for the French, huh?"

"Don't Americans eat bread?" I search for his eyes in the dark.

"At home we eat Wonder Bread." Scott traces a huge W with his flashlight.

"What is so wonderful with your bread?"

"It comes sliced in a plastic bag."

"Then it's for picnics. What do you eat at dinner?"

"The same."

"So you picnic every day?"

"Next time we go to la cabane," Scott says, elbowing me with a gentle nudge, "I'll make you an American picnic."

I'd like that, I think as we walk up rue Principale. Shoppers are running last-minute errands, and the bakery is as crowded as the church on Easter Sunday.

"Let's go to the other bakery," Scott says. I glance at him. He shrugs. "Bread is bread, no?"

"Come on," I say, pushing open the door of Annie's bakery.

"I think it's important to challenge things," Scott says.

"Just don't challenge my mother's taste."

Scott throws his hands up and follows me. Annie stands behind the counter, but when she sees us coming in, she disappears into the back of the bakery.

"That was cold," Scott says in a quiet voice. He gets his baguette and then nudges me. "Your turn."

Madame Duval smiles as usual when she hands me my two baguettes and my change, but her fingers linger for a brief second on mine. "Did something happen that I should know?" Her voice is low when she adds with a small sniffle, "Annie is not talking to me at all, and I'm worried."

"No." I shake my head. "Nothing happened." I tighten my grip around the loaves of bread and leave without another word.

"I feel bad for Annie," Scott says when we are outside.

"Why?" I face him, waiting for an explanation.

"She looks upset. That's all."

"Look, you aren't the one who deals with her bad moods every single day!" I take a deep breath and look straight into his eyes. "And I didn't do anything."

"What do you mean?" Scott holds my stare.

I lower my eyes. "I know that the day we found la cabane you didn't come home until very late."

"So you're spying on me?" Scott kicks a pebble with his sandal. "I never thought of you as a spy."

"It's just that Annie and I were good friends until—"

"I'm complicating your life, right?" Scott's voice slices through the early night with annoyance tinted with sadness. He picks up his pace, his guitar case bumping against his leg.

I know that if I don't say anything now, I will spoil forever what we shared this afternoon.

"That's not what I meant," I say, catching up with him.

Scott stops in his tracks. "Friends don't spy on each other."

His tone of voice is not mean, but it hangs above me as he enters Hollywood Follies, leaving me on the sidewalk with my bread. I hurry home with his words filling my head. I don't like that he thinks I'm watching him, but it doesn't change the fact that he doesn't want to tell me what he did after we found la cabane.

I walk home, thinking of Christmas coming up. Will Annie and I exchange gifts like we have done for the last three years? I can't help thinking I'm losing her friendship because of Scott. Right now I would do anything to get back the life I had before he arrived. It can't happen, yet I can plan Christmas as if Scott hadn't moved here. By the time I enter my home, I've decided that I have to find Annie a unique Christmas gift.

"*Merci, mon chou,*" Maman says as I hand her the bread. "Dinner is almost ready."

"How is Annie?" Papa looks up from his newspaper.

Elle rushes to the cupboard. "I'll set the table," she says, busying herself around the kitchen.

"I haven't seen her in ages," Papa goes on. "You girls are still friends, right?"

"I need to wash up before dinner."

He folds his paper. "What's wrong, *ma puce?*"

Elle hovers in the kitchen like a fly above a pie.

"Nothing's wrong," I say, avoiding Papa's eyes.

He sticks his glasses in his shirt pocket as he walks toward me. He puts his big hand on my shoulder. "Life is full of annoying problems you'll have to deal with sooner than you wish. For now, enjoy life as a kid." He gives a gentle squeeze to my shoulder. "You have no reason to worry."

I shake my shoulder free. "You're wrong! You just forgot what it is to be a kid!"

The clatter of a broken glass startles us. "Sorry." Elle's small face is pinched with apprehension.

"You see what you've done?" Papa says. "Scaring your baby sister."

"I'm eight and a half," Elle says, but when she catches Papa's glare, she bends to pick up the broken pieces.

"*Non!*" Maman says. "You'll hurt yourself! Move away and let me clean up."

My father gets the broom and my mother gets the dustpan. Elle and I are climbing the stairs to our room, Chocolat on our heels, when I hear Papa's broken voice. "I just want the best for her," he says. "You know that, Simone, don't you?"

Maman sighs. "I know, Denis. I know you mean well. But sometimes twelve-year-old girls are hard to reach. I wasn't much different, remember?"

The idea that my parents have known each other for that long freaks me out. The fact that they want to keep Elle and me little kids forever freaks me out even more. I close the door on them and slump on my bed.

"It's okay," Elle says in a voice as soft as a whisper.

"Stop watching me!" Her little face scrunches up. "I'm sorry," I mutter.

"I'll do my Christmas wish list," Elle says. She gets her fancy paper and pen.

As for me, there are just too many feelings that crowd my heart. When I try to express them, words bump against each other. They jam my head and can't find their way to my notebook. I watch Elle hunched at her desk, writing her Christmas wish list.

She just gave me the idea for a perfect gift for Annie.

20 DEATH STINKS

[Scott:]

Why is Sylvie bothering me with her questions about Annie this and Annie that? Since the day I played the guitar for her and she sang me her songs, we haven't talked to each other. I know it would help if I told her where I went after we found this little house in the woods. But a promise is a promise, right?

Anyway, because we haven't met since then, I'm bored and I'm looking forward to seeing Ibrahim. I spot him right away, playing pinball in the back of the café.

"*Quoi de neuf?*" I ask Garçon. I've learned that the French use as many words to greet people as Americans do, and I like to try them out.

"Nothing new, l'américain." Garçon is dusting the picture frames on the shelf behind him. When he's finished, he sets two glasses down on the counter.

"For you and him," he says, jerking his thumb toward Ibrahim.

What's up with this guy? He makes fun of me each time I open my mouth and tolerates Ibrahim only because it would be against the law if he refused to let him in.

Garçon pours golden liquid from a bottle that doesn't have any label. "It's a new drink and I'd like your opinion. Call your friend!"

As I turn to wave Ibrahim to the counter, a man comes in. He tips his black felt hat and crushes his cigarette in an ashtray. In a flash, I see that Garçon brings the bottle and the two glasses down to the sink.

"*Bonjour, Détective,*" he says, his voice thick as honey.

I glance at the man, trying to remember where I've seen him before. He narrows his eyes as if he is also trying to put a name on my face. And that's when I know I've seen him at Chez Lili before. I didn't know he was a cop.

"What can I offer you?" Garçon asks. "A red or white wine? A liquor, maybe?"

"An espresso." The man slides on a stool. He brings one elbow to the counter and cups his chin in his palm.

The espresso machine hisses and steams as coffee fills the cup. "Here you are," Garçon sets the cup before the man.

The detective dips a cube of sugar in the cup and licks the spoon. He turns toward Ibrahim and me.

"How are you, young men?"

"Fine," we say at the same time.

He leans above the counter. "Hey, Garçon, don't tell me you were ready to serve alcohol to the kids."

"No, of course not," Garçon says, all honey gone in his voice. "Calvados can be deceiving and this particular bottle was a bad one."

Ibrahim elbows me. "Let's go."

When I haven't moved, still wondering if Garçon really intended to make us drink alcohol, the detective says, "It's against the law to serve alcohol to anyone who is not sixteen years old."

Ibrahim shoves me to the door, but not before I catch the amused look in the detective's eyes and panic oozing from Garçon.

On the sidewalk, Ibrahim slaps my shoulder. "Garçon can be such a crook."

"Why do you keep coming here, then?" I match my pace to his stride.

"Look," he says, stopping to face me. "You want to be a foreigner forever? That's your problem. Me, I want to blend in. At the Arab teashop, I'll only speak Arabic. I don't want to live in France and drink mint tea and eat couscous for the rest of my life. At Chez Lili, I get some French culture."

"French culture? You've got to be kidding? He wanted to serve us alcohol!"

"Alcohol is forbidden in my religion. So Garçon wants to test me." Ibrahim pokes a finger in my chest. "And you, you're the Coca-Cola boy, so you must pass the same test."

"If he ever comes to my country," I say, narrowing my eyes. "I'll make him a suicide soda."

Ibrahim laughs. "A what?"

"You mix all kinds of sodas," I say, laughing with him. "I'm sure he'll hate that."

Ibrahim makes a face. "You know, Garçon isn't that bad."

Personally? I think the guy's a jerk and his café has a nice name that doesn't fit him at all.

"People are much more than what they seem," Ibrahim goes on.

He lets me digest this information. And in a flash I picture Garçon dusting his picture frames behind the counter. His rag sweeps across them slowly and gently, almost as if he could touch the woman and the little girl behind the frames.

"You watch my game today?" Ibrahim asks.

"Like I've missed any," I say. "Look, we've got time. Want to stop by my place first?"

"Uh," Ibrahim says, but he follows me up the street.

My father has hung a wind chime at the door instead of a traditional bell.

Ibrahim whistles. "*Chouette.*"

The shop smells of patchouli but also of exotic musk from India and Africa; I'm used to it, but Ibrahim's nostrils flare open. He stops by the wooden statues of giraffes and elephants.

"They come from Kenya," I say.

"Have you been to Africa?"

"I've traveled a bit with my parents." I steal a glance at Ibrahim. I know nothing of his family and his neighborhood. He trails his fingers along the back of the elephant and the neck of the giraffe. "Want to see more African art?" I ask.

Ibrahim tags along. "Whoa!" he says when we pass the racks of Levi's, the Hang Ten T-shirts, and the Indian tunics. His hand brushes the clothes as he glances down at his plain corduroy pants and wool sweater.

Dad emerges from behind a stack of boxes. "Oh, hi there," he says, straightening his denim shirt.

"Dad, this is Ibrahim Maarouf, a boy from my class. Ibrahim, this is my father."

"*Enchanté,*" my father says.

"Me, too," Ibrahim says in English. He scratches his head. "That's pretty much all I know." My father laughs and Ibrahim's face breaks into a grin. "I like your shop," he adds in French. I catch Dad's gentle expression on Ibrahim as he eyes the jeans and shirts around us.

Stacey leaps out next to us. "Daddy," she says, pointing at Ibrahim. "I saw him play soccer at recess. He's incredible."

"I'm okay." Ibrahim shifts his weight from one foot to another.

"Okay?" Stacey says, hands on her hips. "You're the best! Last time I—"

"Thanks for sharing, Stacey," I say. "Dad, I'd like

to show my room to Ibrahim."

Dad pats my shoulder. "Sure, son. Anytime."

"*Au revoir, Monsieur,*" Ibrahim says, following me.

"Doug," my father says. "Call me Doug."

Ibrahim whistles again when he enters my room. "What's that?" He points at my baseball bat.

"It's a baseball bat. I used to play back home." I pretend to swing my bat. "And that is my favorite team." I stick my Dodgers cap on Ibrahim's head. "You can keep it, if you'd like."

"Thanks. But won't you miss it?"

"It's all right." In fact, this cap, like a lot of stuff from home, has to go, and only someone like Ibrahim can appreciate it.

Ibrahim paces my room. "This is beautiful," he says, pointing at the medieval tapestry hung in front of my bed. "But it's not from Africa."

"It's from France." That's all I can manage to say, before Mom's face takes up all of the space in my thoughts.

"You said you had never been to France before." Ibrahim trails his fingers along the fabric. "How did you get it?"

"My mom gave it to me." I take a deep breath. "Before she died."

Ibrahim takes his cap off. "She died? That stinks," he says.

I can only nod.

21 A FRENCH ANTIWAR PROTEST

[*Sylvie, December 10, 1970:*]

Rain pelting the roof wakes me up. I pull my blanket up to my nose and stretch out my pajama sleeves. The house is quiet, and, delighted, I remember it is Thursday. No school! I cuddle in the warmth of my bed, wondering if Scott will call and ask me to meet him at la cabane.

It has been awkward between us since he played the guitar and I sang my songs. In a way it's my fault. I asked too many questions. But I can't help thinking that I would still be friends with Annie if Scott hadn't moved to Château Moines.

Besides, the rain will give me time to finish Annie's gift. I grab my box of pens, my colored pencils, and the folder holding my work. Elle is still asleep, buried under a heap of blankets, and I tiptoe downstairs.

I find a note from my parents on the kitchen table. Although they went to the market, they've left the radio on and it's playing a song from this new French kids' band. It's a peace song, and I'm annoyed that it reminds me of Scott. War and peace don't mean much to me, while on the other hand, he can't stop talking about the Vietnam War, as if he was at war himself.

I make myself a bowl of café au lait. Chocolat is polishing off his breakfast with loud slurps. When he hears me, he wags his tail without looking up from his dish.

"Greedy animal," I say.

I spread a thick layer of jam on my bread and read what I wrote last night. *Not bad*, I think, hoping Annie will like my gift. Chocolat perks up his ears and growls.

I recognize the sloshing sound of a pair of rubber boots as a voice calls, "*Bon appétit, ma belle!*"

"Mémé! You scared me!" Chocolat hides behind me.

"Look, stupid dog." Mémé flaps her coat open. "My cat stayed home." Chocolat backs up.

Mémé's red umbrella drips water around her matching rubber boots. Chocolat licks the puddle while she hangs up her raincoat and hat. I fold my papers away. Mémé sits next to me. She fluffs her red hair with one hand and fluffs my hair with the other. Chocolat settles at my feet, one ear up, just in case Blanche Neige, Mémé's cat, jumps from her purse. I can't blame him. Mémé gave her cat the gentle name of Snow White, which doesn't fit the cat that terrorized Chocolat when he was only a puppy.

"Comment ça va, ma belle?" Mémé asks, in a light tone of voice.

"Some coffee, Mémé?" I set her cup on the table.

Mémé's hand, as tiny as Elle's, wraps around my wrist. "How are you?" I steal a glance at my grandmother. "Your mother worries," she goes on. "She finds you distant." She has a small giggle that makes her dimples quiver. "I told her that you have to worry her since you are twelve, but it doesn't seem to reassure her." Mémé shoos Chocolat away with a gentle jab of her heel. She drinks her cup of coffee and helps herself to another one. "So, tell me, *comment ça va?"*

I bury my head in my bowl *"Bien. Et toi?"*

"Me?" She pats her pocket. "Your grandfather keeps me good company and I have my friends. Actually, I stopped by on my way to visit the Colonel. He is getting old, the poor man." I don't dare tell Mémé that she is the Colonel's age.

The phone rings as Elle enters the kitchen. "Mémé!"

I pick up while the two of them coo and cuddle.

"Bonjour, c'est Scott."

Blood swishes in my ears, and I find myself gripping the phone. Why is Scott calling me? Does he want to apologize or admit that something happened with Annie?

"Can we meet?" He has switched to English and his voice sounds urgent.

"It's raining!"

"At the library? Now?"

"Okay," I say, wondering why I can't just say no.

"Your English is improving," Mémé says, with an appreciative nod.

Elle cups her hand around Mémé's ear. "It's because of Scott!" she says, loud enough so I hear.

"Really?" Mémé pats Elle's head. "Tell me, is he a nice boy?"

"Oh, he is *chouette* and his sister too. Stacey is really cool and we …"

Mémé and Elle have always reminded me of two birds, and this morning I find a good title for a potential song: "Gossiping on a Twittering Branch."

I sneak away and get my raincoat. Chocolat trails behind me. "Sorry, no dogs allowed at the library." He tosses anxious glances in Mémé's direction. I pat the top of his head. "Don't worry, Blanche Neige is really home."

Mémé and Elle have switched to confidence mode, and they don't even stop talking when I announce in a loud and clear voice that I'm leaving.

By the time I reach the library I'm drenched, and if it weren't for the tone of Scott's voice, I would dash home right away. I spot him huddling against the library door. Rain trickles from the hood of his poncho.

"Have you watched the news?" he says as I dismount my bike.

"Excuse me?"

"My friend Pete called me," he says. "There have been more antiwar protests everywhere in America."

I peek at his feverish eyes. Is he telling me he ordered me out in the pouring rain just to announce some protests thousands and thousands of kilometers away from Château Moines?

He grabs my wrists with his hands. "We have to do something."

Although it's obvious that he didn't call me to apologize or tell me about Annie, I have the feeling it's no use to argue now. Besides, rain is pelting us. "Can we talk about it inside?"

Warmth and silence welcome us inside the library. We wipe our shoes on the mat and shake our dripping clothes.

"You'll get sick," I say, pointing at Scott's feet, bare in his weird sandals.

"I won't wear any socks until the end of the war," he says, emphasizing each of his words. "That's the least I can do to oppose the worst thing Americans ever did." Pearly drops of rain, reminding me of Christmas lights, edge the fringes of his hair.

"There is always something worse," I say, but when Scott looks at me I shut up.

He pulls me to a table that faces the park. "Look," he says. "I feel so powerless, so worthless, so ... nothing." His breath catches in his throat.

"Hey, it's all right."

"No, it's not and I need to do something. Even if I'm far from home. Even if the French don't care, don't give a—"

"That's not true!" I say. "I was just listening to a peace song when you called."

He chuckles. "Don't pretend that you care about Vietnam!"

"Just because I'm not marching or burning the flag doesn't mean that I like war," I say, squirming in my chair.

I also feel powerless and worthless, and for more reasons than the Vietnam War, if he wants to know. Besides, what can I do about a war? But now isn't the time for arguing so I say, "My country is a land of wars. How couldn't I care?"

"Then, we agree." Scott gets a few crumpled sheets of paper from his jeans' back pocket. He irons them with the flat of his hand. "We need to have our own protest," he says. He pounds the table. "Right here."

"You mean an antiwar rally?"

"Exactly." Scott rewards me with one of his movie-star smiles.

I've got the perfect opportunity to tell him that I have no clue what an antiwar rally is, but I don't take it.

An hour later, we have agreed on May 4th. I should say, Scott decided on May 4th.

"On May 4, 1970," he tells me, "Four students were shot and killed at a peace rally on a college campus in Ohio. We'll march on the same day in 1971 to honor their memory and say no to violence."

I write down the steps of the plan: a march through town leading us to the park, ending with a community picnic in the meadow in the forest.

"Now," Scott says, folding the papers and putting them back in his pocket. "We need to make some fliers and banners." He gives me another of his melting smiles. "You're in charge."

"Me?"

"You're the queen of words."

What can I say when I have shared my entire song notebook with him?

"Besides, you have seen May 1968," Scott says.

"*Un petit peu*," I lie once more. "I saw just a little bit."

"More than enough to be in charge," he says, and I shut up. "We'll need everyone's help, anyway. Kids from school, parents, people in town."

As I digest the information, Mademoiselle Moulin's high-heeled boots cut through the silence. "Scott! Sylvie! What a perfect day to huddle together!"

"We aren't huddling," I say, looking down at my feet.

Scott cups his hands as if spies had infiltrated the library. "We're plotting."

Mademoiselle Moulin pulls up a chair and before long, she knows everything about Scott's plans. "I'll present your project to the CAI," she says, jotting down notes on a pad.

"The what?" I ask, as if she had said a bad word.

"*Centre d'Assimilation pour Immigrants*, the Immigrant

139

Assimilation Center. We try to make it easier for new immigrants. We help them with their paperwork and provide support. I will also approach my book club, my yoga class, my pottery atelier, my …" She sends Scott a radiant smile. "Does your father know about your terrific plan?"

"I'll tell him myself," Scott says. Patches of red appear on his cheeks and neck, and I wonder why he seems so upset all of a sudden.

"Of course," Mademoiselle Moulin says.

She returns to her notes, while Scott scribbles so hard on his paper that he makes a hole in it.

22 PLANNING THE ANTIWAR MARCH

[*Scott:*]

"Scott has told us about his idea for a peace march," Monsieur Leroy says. "May I suggest the event should take place on May 8th instead of the 4th? First, May 8th is a Saturday, meaning more people could participate. Then, it would have a more profound meaning. Who knows why?" He waits for a few seconds. "May 8 marks the end of the Second World War," he goes on, when nobody has said anything. "Do we have any volunteers to help with this project?"

Brigitte jumps in, "I'll design a T-shirt for the marchers."

She hasn't struck me as being politically engaged, so I give her a grateful thumbs-up while Monsieur Leroy writes her name on the board.

"Anyone else?" he asks.

"Who cares?" a boy says from the back. "We live in France. It's the Americans who are at war." A loud stampede of feet accompanies his words.

Monsieur Leroy waves his piece of chalk. "Come on! Let's be civilized people."

"Civilized? As if war is!" Annie leaps to her feet.

"Thank you, Annie for sharing your opinion," Monsieur Leroy says. "Anything you want to do for the march?"

She casts me a dark look. "I work better when I feel trusted. And needed."

"Anyone else?" Monsieur Leroy paces the classroom.

"I can bring a lot of people," Ibrahim says.

Silence, as heavy as the rain that batters the windows, follows his words. I've already understood that the Arabs are known in France for their large families, and that that's one of the many things that upsets the French greatly. Nobody doubts that Ibrahim can bring lots of people. It's just that nobody seems to think that the Arabs should participate.

"Super!" I say, but the same boys in the back shout and whistle until Ibrahim sits down.

"Enough!" Monsieur Leroy says, and he adds Ibrahim's name under Brigitte's. He looks around. "What about you, Sylvie?"

In a quick and quiet voice Sylvie says, "I'll make up a slogan."

"Wonderful," Monsieur Leroy says with a smile. Sylvie doesn't see it, since she keeps her eyes to her desk.

One by one, a few more people volunteer. A

couple of them say they will talk to their church, another boy will talk at catechism, and a girl suggests we visit all the places where adults meet. I plan to take care of Chez Lili myself, and I already feel my stomach churning when I think of Garçon. For the rest of the morning, I stay away from the boys who made the stupid comments, preferring the girls' company.

"I'll ask my brother about the T shirts," Brigitte says at lunchtime. She pokes her fork through her French fries and waves it in the air. "No doubt he'll come up with the best idea."

"No doubt about it!" Annie mimics her, digging her fingers in the platter of fries.

"Use your fork!" Brigitte says. "That is disgusting!"

"Disgusting yourself!" Annie stuffs a fistful of fries in her mouth.

Brigitte's screams alert a cafeteria lady, who hurries over.

"Do you all want lunch detention?"

"Would you like to join us for an antiwar protest?" Brigitte says in a calm voice. "We need lots of people to show our opposition to the Vietnam War."

"Count me in!" the lady says. "Wars cut too many lives short. Our governments should listen to young people and we wouldn't have any wars." She glances at the empty platter of fries. *"Plus de frites?"*

The second helping of fries brings a truce, and by the end of the day a few more kids have signed up.

It has rained all day and it's still raining when

Sylvie and I pick up our sisters at their school at five o'clock. They run ahead of us, jumping and splashing in puddles, some as large as tidal pools. Our sisters are inseparable, and every day Stacey begs for Elle to stay at the store. And every day Sylvie has to remind Elle that their mother wants her home right after school. Today is no exception.

"Please!" Elle imitates a sad dog face. "Pick me up when it stops raining."

"Maman will ground me," Sylvie says.

"Please!"

"It's okay with us," Stacey says.

Sylvie peeks at me. "Are you sure that's okay with your father?"

"Positive," I say, thinking of Mom, who encouraged us to have friends over. "I'll walk her home in time for dinner."

"You could do that?"

How could I refuse, now that Sylvie is so close to me that I can smell her lemony shampoo? "No problem," I say. Today I feel full of convictions. Besides, Sylvie has been avoiding me for so long that it will be cool to be alone for a few minutes. "Also," I say. "I've got to run some errands for dinner. Do you mind if I walk with you?"

She shrugs. I notice different shades of brown that I never saw before in her hair when she pushes it away from her face. "Uh," she says, breaking the silence. "You really think this peace thing is a good idea? Do you believe people will come?"

"Absolutely," I say in my best convincing voice, although I haven't told my father yet. "We'll roll through it."

Monsieur Leroy said we have to contact the mayor and the police. The mayor's son is in our class and he supports the peace march, so we are pretty much covered. But I have to check with the police. When I think of the man with the black felt hat, I wish someone else would ask him.

I'm glad Sylvie agreed to help out. If she hadn't told me about the social riots of May 1968, I wouldn't have even tried our own peace march. She remains silent, and I think that her brain must be churning out words and sentences, as mine is preparing a strong speech to persuade the man with the black felt hat.

23   MAMAN'S CONFESSION

[*Sylvie:*]

How can Scott believe that I'm able to find a slogan for the peace rally? I don't even know what a peace rally is. Is there any way I can get out of this? After all, many kids in our class didn't sign up for anything. I've been so stupid to brag about May '68. If I had kept my mouth shut, I would be just fine. Of course, I haven't said a word to my parents. Except for Papa's monthly union meetings, our political involvement is zero.

While I turn my worries around in my head, I spot Papa pulling the Peugeot into the garage. Despite the heavy rain that drips down my neck, and the fact that I haven't been talking much to him, I wait for my father. Together, we make a mad dash to the front door.

"Come on in!" Maman hands us warm towels and dry socks. "Where is Elle?" she says, staring at me.

"At Stacey's," I say, toweling my hair.

Maman tears the towel from my hands. "What?"

"I'm tired of having to tell her no every day," I say. "Can I have the towel, now?"

"Listen." Maman stuffs the towel against me. "I don't know this family. The boy is barefoot in the winter, the father sells hippie clothes, and nobody has seen a mother."

"She's dead," I say. "Happy?"

"That's terrible," Papa says.

"I'm sorry for their loss," Maman says. "But my point is even more valid. This man is not only running a store but also raising his kids alone. He's too busy to watch over my daughter."

"Is there anything we can do for them?" Papa says, slipping his dry socks on.

Maman balls up the wet towels. "And what exactly are you thinking of?"

"Well." Papa scratches his head. "Maybe having kids over isn't such a bad idea. I'd like that for myself. Kids would take my mind away from my sad thoughts if you were gone."

Maman tightens her lips and disappears into the bathroom. The washing machine's door slams like a slap in my face when she says out loud, "Since they moved here, Sylvie is in and out. She isn't friends with Annie anymore. You can think what you want, but I have my opinions about these people."

"You know what?" I say, following her voice to the bathroom. "These people are great. They are for peace, and Scott is organizing a march against the Vietnam War. Like it or not, I'm part of it!"

Maman wheels around. "What are you talking about?" She turns to my father. "Why don't you say something?"

I steal a glance at Papa. His arms hang limply at his sides, and although I'm still upset when I think of his gifts and the way he wants to overprotect me, I like what he just said. I feel an impulse to reach for his cheek and give him a kiss like I did when I was little, but he walks into the kitchen and I let him go.

"I guess you are right, *ma puce,*" he says from above his shoulder. "People of all ages have worries." Then he says he is picking up Elle himself.

"Do you need help to prepare dinner?" I ask Maman when Papa is gone.

She doesn't answer, but still I pull the plates, the glasses, and the utensils from the cupboard and set them around the table.

"I just worry about you," Maman says, right behind me.

I arrange each napkin next to the knife, just the way my mother likes it.

"This boy, Scott? You spend too much time with him."

I spin around. "Maman! He's a friend!"

"Still. You stopped seeing Annie for him." She wipes her hands on her apron.

"That's not true!" I slam the water pitcher on the table. "Annie is the one who stopped seeing me!"

"Her parents worry. They find her sad and aggressive."

"I have nothing to do with that. She hasn't exactly been nice recently."

"I worry, too. The two of you used to be like that," she says, bringing two fingers together. "I miss it."

I squeeze the salt and pepper shakers. "You miss it? Are you worried for me or for you?"

Words shoot to my brain like the quick sparks of Bastille Day's fireworks. Unlike the fireworks, they are not an anticipation of fun. I rush to my room and drag my trunk from under my bed. I flip my notebook open, get my pen and jot down some ideas;

Don't Rip My Heart, Why Does Love Hurt? Love Me Like I Am, I Dream of Peace, You Never Get It...

A soft knock at my door interrupts me. "Can I come in?" Maman says.

I push the trunk under my bed and hide my notebook under my pillow. "What for?"

"I have something to tell you." Maman props my door open.

I make room on my bed and she sits, arranging the perfect pleats of her skirt.

"When I was your age," she says. "I fell in love with a boy."

"I'm not in love," I say, sucking on my pen.

"My best friend fell in love, too." Maman frowns and sighs, obviously facing a difficult memory. "With the same boy."

"Really?" I say in a flat tone, but I'm getting curious. Most kids who grew up with my parents never left Château Moines, so I wonder if I know the best friend and the boy.

"The boy is your father," Maman whispers. "The girl left."

"Did Papa love the girl?"

"He married me. But I lost my best friend." Before shutting the door behind her, she turns around. "Make peace with your friend before talking of a peace rally."

Her words leave an unpleasant aftertaste in my mouth. My mother's confession pulls me away from the peace rally. I let my family eat dinner without me as words pour out of my mind. I get my notebook from under my pillow and open it to a clean blank page.

Broken friendship. Shattered heart. Crush, smash, wreck…

None of the words make a full sentence, much less a song.

24 A DISTURBING AUDITION AND SOME DIRTY LAUNDRY

[Scott, December 12, 1970:]

We've made some major adjustments to our California lifestyle. Dad bought a secondhand Renault, and every Sunday afternoon we have been driving along the country roads, hoping for the sun to break through the dark rolling clouds. We gave up roller-skating until spring. Stacey got a pair of knee-high rubber boots and I stored my flip-flops away. But I kept my promise and still walk barefoot in my Birkenstocks. The kids at school roll their eyes each morning, but I don't care. I'll prove to them that Americans don't change their minds.

Today Troubadour is having tryouts for his annual Christmas concert. He wants me to audition as a practice test to decide if I can be part of the spring concert. Although I've been playing like a maniac and my fingers have grown calluses, I'm not sure I'm ready. As I'm putting my guitar in its case, I let my thoughts wander.

It has been three months since school started. Mom would be happy to know that I've met some kids and have even convinced them to organize a peace rally. She would be surprised though that I haven't told Dad yet. It seems we are busy without knowing what the other one does.

"Are you ready?" Stacey stands at my door, dressed in her rain gear.

Dad pokes his head above hers. "It's pouring, so I'll drive you to La Clef de Sol."

I don't know how and when, but he and Troubadour met before I got a chance to introduce them to each other. As I expected, the two of them have clicked.

We pile into the Renault. Dad drops me in front of the store while he looks for a parking spot. La Clef de Sol is packed with people I don't know. The store smells of wet wool, tobacco, and perfume. I spot Troubadour in an animated discussion with a man who I only see from the back.

"Hey!" I call when I'm within distance.

At the sound of my voice, Troubadour and his companion turn around. Blood swooshes inside me as I recognize the man with the black felt hat. An amused smile passes over his face. A reed is stuck between his lips, and a saxophone hangs around his neck.

Troubadour acknowledges me with a big smile.

"This is Richard," he says, pointing to the saxophonist, and in a fake menacing voice he adds, "Beware, he's a cop."

"We know each other," Richard says in the same tone. "Right, *petit?*"

I can only nod.

"Then," Troubadour says. "I'll leave you together. I have to greet the company."

No! I want to shout. *Stay!* But Troubadour saunters away.

"So you're a musician," Richard says, glancing at my guitar case. "And also a friend of Troubadour's."

I nod again.

"Call me Richard," he says. "Even policemen have names. And today, I'm here for fun, not for business. So relax, all right?"

I nod once more, but I'm relieved when Troubadour calls for our attention.

"Listen, people," he says. "I don't want to repeat last year's disaster." Laughter interrupts him. "If you don't feel like playing then don't, but if you do want to play, please show up on concert day." More laughter and whistles accompany his words.

One by one the musicians play their pieces and then shake hands with Troubadour instead of signing a formal agreement. When most of the people have left, Troubadour asks me to play my piece. I tune my guitar, plucking the strings to make sure it is in tune. Although the store is almost empty, I still feel nervous. Blood beats like a drum inside my chest and head. I clear my throat and take a deep breath.

"It's my pleasure to play for you 'We Can Work It Out' by the Beatles."

"Bravo!" Stacey jumps from her chair.

I start singing; my voice is a bit shaky at first but gets more confident as I let the music carry me away. I try to forget that people are listening to me. Instead, I think of how four British guys wrote these lyrics without knowing that a California boy would play the guitar and sing their song to French people, who are probably not getting every word. At some point I hear the sound of the doorbell, but nothing can stop me.

When I'm finished, I take a bow. Richard is making the thumbs-up sign. He's not that intimidating for a cop, now that I know he's a musician, too. I put my guitar away as the last people mingle, drinking coffee or smoking cigarettes.

"Bravo, Scott," Troubadour says, slapping my shoulder. "You'll be a fine addition to the Christmas concert."

"Christmas?"

Troubadour makes his little salute. "Same song, same place."

My father pats my back. "Good performance, son!"

"Thanks, Dad. Troubadour wants me to play next week."

"Great!" My dad's eyes shine with pride and true excitement.

I'm light as a bubble and I say, "I'm also organizing a peace rally against the Vietnam War on May 8th. We'll march through town, play music, have food and—"

"What a terrific idea!" Dad sounds really excited. "Tell me more about it." But all of a sudden he's not looking at me anymore, and I follow his gaze. Mademoiselle Moulin is standing a foot away from my father.

"*Sophie! Comment ça va?*"

She kisses my father on both cheeks. "*Bien, merci, Doug. Et toi?*"

So he knows her name is Sophie and they are using the familiar "*tu*," and they kiss? The pride of being part of the concert is fading away, and when Stacey pulls my sleeve, I push her away more roughly than I intend. I grab my guitar case and hurry to the door, Stacey on my heels.

"You stay here," I say. "I'm walking home."

"But it's raining!" My little sister looks panicked.

"I won't die." Stacey shrinks in her holiday velvet dress. I want to hug her, but instead I leave.

It all has happened so fast that I forgot my rain jacket in the store, but I'd rather get pneumonia than return for it. The beating of the rain matches my rage. What is Dad doing with this woman? Gosh, I feel so angry that I'm glad I left.

Mom loved teaching us French idioms. One of them spares me the embarrassment of a scene at La Clef de Sol: "*On doit toujours laver son linge sale en famille*"

155

or in English, "You should wash your dirty laundry at home." As I ruminate about how I will make sure that Dad and I do that, I've arrived downtown.

My sweater and my feet are soaking wet, my guitar weighs a ton, and Chez Lili has never looked so cozy. The smells are now as familiar as the ocean's salty air was only four months ago. Ibrahim waves from the back when he sees me. Even Garçon juts his chin in my direction, and I return his silent greeting the same way.

"How did it go?" Ibrahim asks, pushing the Dodgers cap away from his eyes.

"Okay." I slip out of my sweater. My T-shirt sticks to my skin.

Ibrahim cups his hands around his mouth and shouts, "One *grog!*"

"*L'américain* is cold?" Garçon says.

Thirty seconds later, I sip the hottest drink I have ever drank. Soon, I feel warm inside and outside. "What's a *grog?*" I ask Ibrahim.

"You don't want to know," he says with a grin. "Kind of a French suicide drink."

"Ooooh!" I say, feeling all giddy and fuzzy.

25 A CHRISTMAS CONCERT ENDING ON
A BITTER TONE

[Sylvie, December 19, 1970:]

Tonight is the Christmas concert at La Clef de Sol. Maman and I haven't missed one since I turned nine. It's our own Christmas kickoff. Scott has passed out invitations in class, announcing his participation. Maman glanced at the names on the invitation and dropped it in the drawer where she keeps the bills. Since then she hasn't said a word about the concert.

In a way, I don't mind that much. If I go, I might bump into Annie. And definitely into Scott. I can't stop envy creeping inside me when I realize that he auditioned only three months after he moved here, while nobody even knows I write songs and I have been here my whole life. I know I'm entirely responsible for keeping it a secret, but I wasn't expecting to feel hurt when I read his name on the program. So if Maman doesn't want to go, for her own reasons, it's fine with me.

After dinner, Papa leaves for his monthly union meeting. I help Maman to clear the table and wash the dishes.

"Your father left us the car," Maman says. She wears a nice blouse and skirt beneath her housedress, and I notice her pair of Sunday earrings. "If we hurry, we still can go to the winter concert."

"Can I go, too?" Elle says.

"I didn't get to go until I was nine," I say.

"Let me call Mémé," Maman says. "She'll babysit you."

"Not fair." Elle stampedes out of the kitchen.

I've changed in a pair of wide-legged black corduroy pants and a white turtleneck sweater before Maman hangs up the phone. I hear her say, "Oh! Too bad. Don't worry, she'll understand. *Bonsoir.*"

"What's wrong?" I ask, while I brush my hair, using the mirror in La Boutique.

"Your grandmother's cat ate something that doesn't agree with her."

"Don't tell me we can't go to the concert because of Blanche Neige!"

At the name of Mémé's cat, Chocolat hides behind me, moaning. "Hush," I say.

"It means I have to go," Elle says, putting her coat on.

Maman finds the last parking spot on the street and squeezes in between two cars. From the back seat, Elle announces that she sees Stacey and Doug.

"Don't call him *Doug*," Maman says, turning the ignition off. "He's an adult, not a child your age. And certainly not a family friend."

Elle rolls her window down and calls out loudly to them.

"*Bonsoir*, Stacey," Maman says when we reach them. "*Monsieur*," she adds with a small nod.

"Please, call me 'Doug,'" he says. He extends his hand, which Maman shakes.

"*Bonsoir, Monsieur.*"

Embarrassed, I hurry inside La Clef de Sol and pick a seat between two women I don't know. From the corner of my eye, I watch Elle, Stacey, and her father taking their seats in the front row. Maman makes her way towards me.

"I couldn't find two seats," I lie.

She wrinkles her brow but manages a smile. "It's all right, I'll get one back there."

The store smells of fresh coffee and hot chocolate. Troubadour has also set up a Christmas tree. Strings of colorful lights run along the walls. Laughter, talk, and the tuning of the instruments sound like a weird but cozy conversation, and I settle in my chair, observing the latecomers.

Mademoiselle Moulin shows up, a colorful shawl thrown over her shoulders. Golden loops dangle at her earlobes. She squeezes in an extra chair so she can sit with Stacey and her father. Ibrahim arrives alone and slides into a chair two rows ahead of me. Brigitte strolls in, wearing a suede maxi coat hemmed with fake fur. Many of my classmates and even Monsieur Leroy and his wife make it here tonight. I crane my neck to check if Annie is here too, but I can't spot her.

When the store is packed, Troubadour claps his hands to get our attention. *"Mesdames, Mesdemoiselles, Messieurs, bonsoir."* He raises his cup of coffee. *"A la musique!"*

"To music!" people shout.

A pianist opens the concert, followed by an accordionist. I glance at the program. Scott is scheduled to play after a harpist, after intermission. A little girl with an Indian flute plays next, and a group of children from the elementary school accompany her with various percussion instruments. Troubadour's performers are diverse, and before I know it, it's time for the intermission.

I stretch my legs in the aisle and glance behind me. Maman is applying a fresh coat of lipstick. I slip back and sit next to her. She gives me a quick but kind look and finishes her touch-up.

When the harpist plays after intermission, Maman leans in toward me. "It's beautiful," she says in a soft voice. "I wish I could play or sing like any of them."

I wish I could tell her right here and now that I actually write songs. But words don't want to leave the cocoon of my head; Maman returns to her program, and the moment is gone.

Scott is next. He steps on stage with his guitar

strapped across his chest. Troubadour dims the spotlights and Scott gives us the first chords of "We Can Work It Out." It's a familiar song; the Beatles have been so popular in France that the whole room knows the melody and hums along. The applause drowns out the last note.

"*Merci beaucoup,*" Scott says, when the clapping has quieted down.

"*Bravo! Bravo!*" I'd recognized my father's voice among hundreds.

I stretch my neck and spot him in his big brown anorak, which makes him look like a bear. He claps, looking around, searching for familiar faces. When he sees me, he makes a small wave in my direction and I wave back, feeling all happy and warm.

A saxophonist ends the concert. Then everybody rushes to get a cookie and a drink, and that's when I catch a glimpse of Annie. Right now, when we aren't in school and when the music makes all of us happy, would be the perfect time to talk to her, but instead I make a mad dash to the door. A few musicians are outside, smoking as they tap their feet to keep them warm. I look for Scott, but he's the one who sees me.

"Thanks for coming," he says. His guitar case sits at his feet.

"You were good," I say.

"You are as good. Why weren't you part of the concert?" He searches my eyes and it makes me feel uncomfortable.

I'm afraid, I want to say, but the little voice that

begs me to stay away from any challenge gets more urgent, imploring me to tuck my thoughts into a safe corner of my head, and I shut up.

"Your songs are great," Scott insists. "As good as many we heard. Several are much better. Why don't you want people know about them?" I want to bring my hands to my ears to block out Scott's words when I hear his last comment. "How do you expect to become a songwriter, much less a singer, if you keep hiding?"

"A songwriter? A singer? Whoa, that's impressive," Annie has joined us without my noticing. I freeze as if Annie had thrown a bucket of ice cubes on my shoulders.

But when I turn and face her, what I read in her eyes isn't sarcasm, but a simple question: *Why does he know this about you and I don't?*

I think of the gift I've made for her. Wrapped in silk paper and tied with a golden bow, it sits, perfect, on my desk. But none of the words that poured from my pen to the paper seem right anymore, now that Annie stands in front of me. I want to tell her that I shared my songs with Scott because I know of his loss and I wanted him to feel less lonely, but Annie has not even known her parents who abandoned her when she was born. So I remain mute, torn between my two friends.

"Listen," Scott starts.

Annie puts her hand up. "Don't bother. I don't care."

I listen to the sloshing sound of her boots on the wet pavement until the night swallows it.

"She's mad," Scott says. "You two should really make peace before Christmas."

Laughter and wishes for a Joyeux Noël can be heard as we walk to the cars. I want to believe Scott and listen to his advice. But when I catch his furious glare at Mademoiselle Moulin, who is talking to his father, I know he is far from being at peace with himself.

26 A TORMENTED HEARTTHROB

[*Scott:*]

"*M on pote*," Ibrahim tells me over a Perrier on Sunday afternoon, "the concert was *chouette*."

"What's a *pote?*" I rack my brain for the French slang words I've learned.

"A pal," Ibrahim says in English. I envy him, for he also speaks Arabic. He nods his head to the beat of one of those French songs I can never remember. "Very cool, the concert, really," he goes on in English.

It was great to play along with other people, but I haven't been able to push back the vision of the librarian sitting next to my father and then leaning in toward him.

When I see Ibrahim's puzzled face, waiting for a comment from my part, I say, "Yeah, it was cool." I guzzle my diabolo menthe. My favorite French drink, made with a mix of French lemonade and mint syrup, it has replaced my beloved Coca-Cola.

"May I join you?" Richard has just come in, and eyes the free chair across from me.

Ibrahim shrinks in his seat and looks sideways, as if expecting danger.

"You're a good saxophonist," I tell Richard, to break the ice.

He lights his cigarette. "For a beginner, you're a pretty decent guitarist, too."

"I used to play back home, but I kind of quit."

"Stuff happens," Richard says in a quiet voice. "It's great that you gave music a second chance."

Garçon sets an espresso in front of Richard. "Lucky is the man who finds a second chance and grabs it," Garçon says to no one in particular, his glazy eyes resting on the photos behind the counter.

Next to me, Ibrahim squirms, checking his watch constantly. "Couscous night," he says, and he sneaks away.

"Another diabolo, l'américain?" Garçon says.

The distinct tapping of a cane signals the Colonel's arrival. "It's on me, then," the Colonel says, as he joins our table. "I heard I missed a good concert."

"Thank you for the drink, Colonel," I say when Garçon brings us the glasses.

"*Pffft,*" he says. "I'm thirsty."

Maybe, now that I can pass for a decent guitarist, it's my chance to tell people about the peace rally.

"Umm, umm," I say, clearing my throat. "At

school, some of us came up with the idea of a peace march to protest the Vietnam War."

The Colonel sets his glass down and raps the ground with his cane. "Whoever thinks that marching can change anything about Vietnam doesn't know anything about wars."

Richard crushes his cigarette in the ashtray. "Don't ever start smoking, *petit*," he says. "Now, for this march, no offense, but the Colonel is right. Do you really think that marching in Château Moines will stop the war in Vietnam?"

They look at me as if, because I'm not yet thirteen and a newcomer, I don't get it. I grab my glass and finish it in a gulp.

"Look, *petit*," Richard says. "I respect your idealism, but here we live in peace, and I doubt people will march against a war thousands of kilometers away from home."

I jump to my feet and catch my glass before it crashes to the ground.

The Colonel grabs my sleeve. "Anger is not the answer."

I jerk my arm away. "Thanks for your support." I'm on my way out so fast that Garçon doesn't get a chance to give me his usual, "Ciao, l'américain."

My anger at both the Colonel and Richard is gnawing at my stomach. I enter the bakery to get some gum. At least I will have something to chew on. Annie is helping a customer, and she stiffens when she sees me. *Good*, I think, *someone else who is mad at me.*

On any other given day, I would leave, but after all, I have nothing to feel guilty about, so I wait as Annie rings up her customer.

Her eyebrows shoot up when I step to the counter. "Can I get a pack of gum?"

"One *franc*," she says, slamming the pack on the counter.

I slide the exact change into the dish and get the gum. I unwrap one stick and ball up the wrapping paper. Annie points to the wastebasket behind her. I aim and miss. A mocking smile purses her lips. I pick up the wrapping paper and score.

"Happy?" I say. Flickers of irritation dance in Annie's green eyes. I attack my piece of gum with all the strength my teeth have. "Do you also think that a peace march is stupid?" I ask.

"It's not like you've asked for my opinion," Annie says.

The doorbell rings as a customer enters. Madame Duval arrives from the back of the store.

"*Bonjour*, Scott," she says. "Thanks for your help Annie, I'll take over."

Without a word and with a stiff back, Annie marches to the door. I follow her down the street and she picks up her pace.

"Hey, there is no reason for being angry," I say when I've caught up with her. "It's not like anyone else knows much about the rally anyway."

Without any warning Annie stops and I bump into her. "Really?" she says, her eyes shooting darts.

"That's not the impression I have."

"What are you talking about?" I push my hands deep in my pockets. My fingers meet Mom's earring and curl around it.

We stand in the middle of the sidewalk and shoppers sigh, annoyed, as they avoid us. Annie motions to a bench. She sits as far away as possible from me.

"Sylvie and I, we were together every Saturday afternoon until she decided I wasn't good enough for her." She sends me a dark look. "I was upset that Saturday when she didn't show up. I told you I like to go to the forest when I want to be alone. So I went for a walk." She twists a strand of hair between her fingers.

"I didn't know." I'm pretty sure Sylvie never told me she spent Saturdays with Annie.

She shakes her head. "How would you feel if your best friend stood you up for someone you took to the very same place before?"

"I had no idea," I say, annoyed that she can be so unforgiving, but also embarrassed that I'm the reason the girls aren't best friends anymore.

"I'm telling you," Annie says with a smirk. "That stinks. On top of it, Sylvie doesn't talk about it, as if it could go away like you erase a blackboard."

"She's doesn't say much, that's all."

"You like her, right?"

"Gee, I thought we were talking about the antiwar march."

Annie's smirk morphs into a small smile. "I suppose you're right." She slides closer to me. "If we decide to organize a peace rally, we better make peace ourselves before that." She extends her hand.

"I thought everybody kissed in France," I say.

"Not for business," Annie says. I shake her hand and she points to her right cheek, which I kiss. "For friendship," she adds, lowering her eyelids.

"Hey," I say as an idea grows in my mind. "Tomorrow's Christmas Eve. I haven't done my shopping yet. Do you want to join me? I'll pick you up at 10 o'clock."

"I haven't done my shopping either," Annie says. With a side-looped smile, she adds, "For a guy who isn't totally fluent in French, you're pretty good with girls. You must have been a Don Juan back home."

Pete and Mike would laugh until they fall to the ground if they heard of my heartthrob reputation in France. I feel like cracking up too, but instead, with the appropriate tired sigh of a real seducer, I say, "You've no idea."

27   A BITTER CHRISTMAS EVE

[Sylvie, December 24, 1970:]

Christmas isn't the same this year. Annie's gift rests on my desk, reminding me of the disaster after the concert. I haven't found or even thought of any gifts for my family. It hasn't snowed yet, although the sun hasn't pierced the white sky for days. It's Christmas Eve, but I don't feel any excitement, any expectation. The radio hums some old holiday songs, and Papa and Maman are having breakfast.

"You're an early bird," Papa says, making room for me at the table.

"I have my shopping to do," I say on an impulse.

"Do you need a ride?" He lowers his tone of voice. "Père Noël is behind on his shopping, too."

"Thanks, but I'll walk." I butter my piece of baguette and spread apricot jam on top.

"You'd better hurry, then. They say we could get

more than five centimeters of snow by noon."

Through the bare trees of our yard, the sky appears low and bulky. I really hope for snow. For some reason, I think snow would clean up the mess of the last weeks.

"I'll be on my way, too," Maman says. "I'm meeting Mémé at the hair salon."

"Meanwhile I'll take care of the tree with Elle," Papa says. Maman brings him a cup of steaming coffee. "*Merci, mon amour,*" he says with a tender smile. I look away.

The phone's ring stops the gooey sentimentality. "For you," Papa says. A small smile makes its way to his lips when he hands me the phone.

"Hey, this is Scott. Want to do your Christmas shopping with me? 10 o'clock at Chez Lili." In a hushed voice, he adds that he has a surprise for me, and he hangs up.

I don't know what to think. On the one hand, I'm glad not to be alone on Christmas Eve. On the other hand, I worry about the surprise he spoke about. I have no gift for him. I miss Annie, and I feel as sentimental as my father when I slip her gift in my bag. Maybe, I could stop by the bakery after I'm finished shopping.

Outside, the air is thick with the anticipation of snow, and I hurry to Chez Lili. Scott is waiting for me. He wears a bulky parka on top of his army jacket, his usual woolen hat, a scarf tied several times around his neck, and a pair of red knitted mittens.

"You'll still get pneumonia," I say, shaking my head at the sight of his weird sandals.

"I won't wear socks until the end of the war," he says, curling his toes.

"That was when you lived in warm California; it doesn't count now."

"No way." He stomps his feet and grabs my arm. "Come on." I follow him, envying his determination.

Rue Principale bursts with activity. Shoppers bundled up in bulky coats and furry boots crowd the sidewalk. Electric trains and animated marionettes decorate the windows of every shop. Holiday music seeps from the streets' loudspeakers. It's hard to resist the excitement, and a smile comes to my lips, as if I was tickled from inside.

"They say it will snow," Scott says, with a happy light in his eyes. "I think I'll get Stacey a sled and get Dad a couple of records."

"Don't you think that's what Troubadour might give him?"

Scott chews on his lip. "Good point. What are you getting your father?"

"A couple of records," I say. "But he isn't friends with Troubadour."

"And for Elle?"

"The sled is a good idea, if you don't mind."

Scott bows. "Be my guest."

We are approaching the bakery, and a pang of nostalgia for last year hits me. At that exact second Annie bounds outside.

"I told you I had a surprise for you," Scott says.

Annie freezes when she sees me. "You didn't tell me *she* was the surprise."

"Same here," I say. I squeeze my bag against my side.

We both look at Scott, who grabs our hands. "Today is peace day," he says.

I glance at Annie. A blue hat hides her eyes, and her cheeks are rosy from cold and embarrassment. She peeks at me. Our eyes meet, and it makes us smile. I consider pulling her gift from my bag, but I don't want to hurt Scott's feelings.

"*Joyeux Noël,*" I say.

"*Joyeux Noël,*" Annie says. She pokes her gloved fist into Scott's ribs. "I've got the peace virus," she says. "Happy?"

"I'm glad I passed it to you."

"Sure," Annie says, but her tight mouth and cold eyes don't match the cheerfulness of her voice.

We've reached Hollywood Follies. Exotic clothes and accessories fill the decorated windows. American holiday songs play through the door, left ajar.

"Huh," Scott says. "We've got lots of new stuff at the store. Want to have a look?"

"Why not?" Annie says. "I've got to find gifts for my foster parents. That's all I need this year."

If Scott believes that Christmas Eve is reason enough for Annie to make peace with me, he doesn't know anything about girls. Her sideways glances in my direction hurt like paper cuts. Although her gift,

173

tucked in my bag, is as light as a feather, its weight crushes me. Last year, Annie and I shared grilled chestnuts that we bought on the street. This year, I've lost my best friend. I don't want to lose my happy memories, and I'd give anything to be the girl I was before, and I know that Scott is the reason I can't be.

"I'll pass," I say. "It's not like Hollywood Follies is the only store in town. Besides, I've done my Christmas shopping without it until now."

Scott shrinks into his coat and he curls his toes, which are blue from the cold. I want to take back what I said, but it's too late. Words full of fury whack my head, and when they come to my lips, they taste of jealousy and resentment. But I'm too proud to back up.

"*Salut,*" I say. I wheel around, just in time to avoid Mademoiselle Moulin, stepping out of the store. Gifts wrapped in colorful holiday paper overflow her bags.

"*Joyeux Noël,*" she says with a big smile when she spots the three of us.

Scott doesn't even look at her as he pulls Annie inside the store. Before the door closes behind them, Annie glances over her shoulder. She mouths something that sounds like, "*Joyeux Noël,* anyway."

I stand alone on the sidewalk as people hurry around me. The first snowflakes tumble down and land on my hair, but the anticipation of snow has left me. In no time, the snowflakes fall, as big as miniature crepes, and the sky closes on Château Moines. In two sentences, I've hurt the boy who wanted me to be friends with Annie again, and I haven't been able to make peace with her. I can't find a single word to describe my feelings. I suppose that some words are as hard to hear in any language, and I want to slam my hands against my ears to quiet the angry lyrics that grow louder and louder inside me.

Snow feels like tears falling from the sky, yet when I see Madame Duval arranging fancy bûches de Noël, cakes shaped like Yule logs, in the bakery window, an urge makes me enter the store.

"Sylvie!" She steps from behind the counter. "Annie wasn't sure she would see you before Noël." She hands me one small pink box. "This is for your sister. Annie says Elle loves meringues. She baked a batch just for her. And this is for you."

My gift has the shape of a book and is wrapped in paper the color of the sky. Annie has written the names of singers and titles of songs all over it.

"*Merci*," I say. I dig in my bag. "This is for Annie. *Joyeux Noël.*"

Madame Duval takes the gift from my hand and slides it beneath the counter. "I'll make sure to give it to Annie. *Joyeux Noël*, Sylvie."

The street, the sidewalks, and the roofs are coated with snow, and Château Moines looks like a fancy cake, iced with white frosting. I feel it impossible not to believe in the hope of peace when everything is white and silent.

Maybe, it's not too late.

28 MERRY CHRISTMAS, L'AMÉRICAIN!

[*Scott:*]

A sheet of flurries slams against my face. The cars creep along rue Principale as slowly as the tanks in the Vietnam jungle, and I crawl like a blind soldier toward our apartment. People around me carry their gifts and Christmas trees home. They laugh and joke when they slip and slide along the sidewalk, but their good mood doesn't change the fact that I feel like a wreck.

Sylvie blames me for being the newcomer who stole her friend. She tried hard to hurt me and it worked. As if that wasn't enough, I bumped into the librarian. Thinking of her is like a splinter jabbed in a thumb. At least Annie, being Annie, didn't try to make me feel better, even when I told her a little bit about Mom.

"Don't feel so special," she said. "I don't even know who my parents are."

So, here I am, holding onto Stacey's sled and the French cookbook I picked out for Dad, since Annie convinced me it was a classic. Maybe Dad will find new recipes or at least new ways of making pasta. As I get closer to Hollywood Follies, I notice a loud group of shoppers in front of the store.

"Scott!" My father, Stacey, and Troubadour wave at me with so much excitement that they seem to have more than two arms each.

"Have you ever seen anything as beautiful as this snowfall?" Dad says.

He wears his red Christmas hat with the white pompom that jingles at the top like a bell. I don't feel like being overfriendly, as the librarian still troubles my mind, but I'm glad Dad's in a good mood.

"Do you want some hot cocoa?" Stacey asks.

Troubadour hands her a ladle. "Your father had the idea," he says, with a pat on my shoulder.

"This is a very nice idea," a woman I've never seen before tells me. "I'm the butcher's wife," she adds, when she sees my blank face.

"I agree," the flower shop owner says, with a warm smile in my direction.

Dad greets shoppers and business owners alike and invites them to have a cup of coffee or hot chocolate. "The Duvals have brought cookies," he tells me, as more people stop by.

"Ooooh!" Stacey slams her hand over her mouth when she discovers the decorated cookies. She eats one and shakes the crumbs off her mittens. Despite everything, I'm happy for my little sister. She deserves a real holiday season.

A car is snaking its way along the street, honking and flashing its lights. Everyone answers with excited screams. The driver stops and rolls his window down. A cigarette dangles at the corner of his mouth. I haven't seen Richard since he gave me his point of view about the peace walk. I'm not sure I want to talk to him right now.

"Come on!" Troubadour calls. "Have a drink with us."

"Coffee or hot chocolate," Dad adds. "I don't want any trouble with the French police."

Richard laughs. Once he has parked his car, he steps over, and Stacey offers him a cup of cocoa. "*Merci, mademoiselle,*" he says, and my sister beams.

He tips his black felt hat when he sees me and walks over, bracing against the snow that the sky dumps on us. "*Comment ça va, petit?*" He looks around and clears his throat. "This peace march of yours?" he says. "What's happening with it?"

"What are you talking about?" I say. A gust of wind blows Richard's hat away. Instinctively, I run and get it.

He mumbles a quick *merci*. "It seems that after all people here like doing things together. So I'll give you the green light. I'll provide security on that day. Go for it." He lights a new cigarette. "Remember, don't start smoking."

Snow spins like a crazy top above our heads. A

few kids roll snowballs. Stacey joins them, and soon a snowball fight starts in the middle of the street. I let Richard finish his cup of hot cocoa while his words sink in.

"Thanks," I say. "For the rally."

"Thanks for the hat," he says and he walks away.

Troubadour says something to my dad and that makes them both laugh. I'm glad for my father that he's making friend miles away from home, but now I need to be alone.

My coat is drenched and my feet are freezing, but I think of the soldiers who are falling under the gunshots at this exact minute and how they must feel to die so far from home, and I stop feeling sorry for myself.

Although it's only six o'clock, the street is deserted except for our small party, and Chez Lili is a lighthouse guiding me through the storm. Warm air, the smell of coffee, and the sound of music welcome me inside.

"Salut, l'américain," Garçon says with half a smile. He stands, as always, between his shelf of photos and his counter.

"Can I get something warm?" I ask.

He pours some water in a cup.

"Water?"

"Stop complaining." He jerks his thumb toward my regular window booth, ordering me to sit down.

I slip my coat off and drop onto the seat. I take my sandals off and sit cross-legged, tucking my numbed feet under my thighs to warm them up.

Garçon brings the cup to the table. "Careful, it's hot." I sip some of the colorless beverage. "So?" He raises one eyebrow.

Warmth fills my stomach, and soon I can wiggle my toes. "Good grog," I say. I catch his surprised look. "It's what you call this hot water flavored with alcohol, right?"

"Right. But don't worry. This is hot mulled cider. Better than a soda, isn't it?" A smile plays behind his mocking smile.

"It's 100% better and the perfect choice on a cold Christmas Eve," I say, and a real grin breaks through his face.

Garçon sits across from me. "By the way, shouldn't you be home with your family on Christmas Eve?"

"They're having a block party." I take a swig of my drink. "What about you?"

His gaze floats around the café and then follows the snowflakes that rush toward the windows, as if they couldn't resist the attraction of light. "I don't like company on certain days," he says.

"Still, it's Christmas Eve. You want to join us?" Garçon doesn't answer. I slide my coat on. "Really," I insist. "You can come."

He jumps at the sound of my voice. "No, no, it's all right. Thank you. *Joyeux Noël*, l'américain, or 'Merry Christmas' like they say in your country."

"Merry Christmas, Garçon."

He shakes his head when he spots my feet. "You'll die of pneumonia."

"I made a promise," I say. "No socks until the end of the Vietnam War."

He shakes his head once more. "Then, pray for a short winter."

"I stopped praying, too," I say.

"I'll pray for you, then." He turns his back to me and rearranges his picture frames.

Snow has stopped, and a few stars shine brightly in the sky like silent firecrackers. Every shop has closed. I remember that we've decided to decorate the tree together, like we did with Mom on Christmas Eve. I hurry up along the street, impatient to be with my family.

A rusty yellow VW Bug is parked in front of the store. I press my body against the window and watch the librarian, arms loaded with wrapped boxes, ring our bell.

29 JOYEUX NOËL

[*Sylvie, December 25, 1970:*]

Joyeux Noël! Joyeux Noël! Joyeux Noël! Joyeux Noël! Mémé hands each of us a Christmas gift. "Did I miss anyone?"

Chocolat pokes his nose out from behind the sofa. Mémé throws him a plastic bone with a red bow taped on top. Chocolat backs up with a moan.

Mémé rolls her eyes. "*Joyeux Noël* to you, too," she says to him. "Ungrateful one."

Elle tears open her gift. Paper and ribbons fly above her head. "Merci, Mémé!"

In a flash I recognize the name of Hollywood Follies on the label. I dig my nails into my palm to keep myself from running to my room and pouring my heart out into my notebook. *Bittersweet* would be a good starting word for a new song.

Elle shows off in a colorful embroidered Indian tunic. "Oh! This is beauuuutiful!"

"This new boutique," Mémé says, bringing her hands to her heart. "It's a treasure chest. And the owner is so nice!"

"Stacey is also very nice!" Elle adds, slipping the tunic on top of her shirt.

Mémé sends me a teasing smile. "Open yours!"

I don't need to check the tag to know that she has done all of her shopping at Hollywood Follies. I should be excited too, since I receive my first pair of Levi's, a T-shirt that says "Hang Ten" on the front, and an assortment of silver bracelets.

"You've spoiled the girls," Maman says, when I don't comment on my gifts.

"Not only the girls!" Mémé says. "Open yours!"

I notice a flicker of hesitation in Maman's eyes as she unties the bow.

"Very unique." Papa says, when Maman unveils a pair of glimmering earrings and a matching necklace.

"Handmade by an artisan in Nepal," Mémé says. "Doug picked them himself."

Maman stiffens, but she kisses Mémé twice on her cheeks. "You shouldn't have."

Mémé waves her away with a quick "*Pfft,*" which she must have learned from the Colonel, but she beams.

We spend the rest of the morning ooohing and aaahing over the rest of our gifts. Although I don't like to be reminded of Scott, I have to admit that Mémé's gifts are the best. Even Papa loves his gift—a pillow she picked out for his favorite TV chair. The names of Hollywood's stars are written all over it, and Papa practices his English by reading them aloud.

My special gift, however, is the one from Annie. She bought me a thick blue notebook, and on the first page she wrote, "*Pour mon amie Sylvie, la reine des mots.*"

The queen of words? That's also what Scott told me. It's funny how both seem to be more aware of my skills than I am. I tuck the notebook into my trunk, hoping Annie likes my gift as much as I like hers.

After the foie gras on toasted bread, the turkey with chestnuts, and the bûche de Noël, Papa yawns. He fluffs his new pillow and gets ready for a nap. The phone jolts Chocolat awake; he had fallen asleep while chewing on his new bone.

I pick up the call. "Thanks for the gift," Annie says. "I love your poems. You really are the queen of words." Her voice is light and soft like a snowflake, and I feel that maybe we are maybe friends again.

"Thanks for your gift, too," I say. "And thanks for calling."

The line is silent for a second. "I hope we can still be friends," Annie says.

"Me too." I want to tell her so much more, but the line crackles, and she's gone.

The phone rings again, and when I recognize Scott's voice I hang up. "Wrong number," I say, but the phone rings again.

"Let me deal with that," Papa says in a sleepy voice.

I'm quicker and hang up for the second time, but not before hearing, "Please, come over. To the store."

Although I don't want to see Scott, I've got the feeling something's wrong if he calls me on Christmas Day.

"I feel like talking a walk," I tell Maman.

"I'll do the dishes," Mémé says. "Go!" She shoos me away with the dish towel.

Maman walks me to the door. "Your grandmother was very generous," she says. "Didn't you get the jeans of your dreams?"

"I like your gifts too." I wave my mittened hands in front of her face.

"Thank you." She wraps my scarf twice around my neck. "*Joyeux Noël,*" she says before she closes the door on Papa's and Chocolat's snoring.

Last night was so cold that the snow that fell yesterday hasn't thawed. It reaches my calves. A pale sun filters through the branches, which crack under the weight of ice. My boots crunch through the snow, but the only sound I hear is Scott's urgent voice, still ringing in my ears. I catch glimpses of flickering lights and glimmering ornaments on the Christmas trees in each house. The shops are closed on rue Principale, but the lights are on in every window, and I feel like I've stepped inside one of those old-fashioned snow globes.

Scott is waiting under the awning of Hollywood Follies. He wears all his winter gear, which makes him look like the Michelin man, and he straddles a sled.

He doesn't have socks on, and it makes me smile that he thought of using a sled to spare his feet.

"Come on," he says. "We've got to go."

"*Joyeux Noël* to you, too," I say.

"Sorry. *Joyeux Noël*." He pats the sled. "Come on."

"Where are we going?"

"To la cabane."

"No way," I say. "It's too far with so much snow." I search for his eyes. "Why do you want to go to la cabane?"

Scott leads the sled to the street. "Are you my friend or not?"

He doesn't wait for my answer, but starts pushing through the snow. I figure that the faster I push, the sooner we'll get there.

It's freezing inside la cabane, but Scott hands me a poncho and a blanket, and I wrap myself around them. He does the same and drops onto a pillow.

"I've got to tell you something," he says, draping an extra blanket on top of our shoulders.

My heart is a battlefield, with questions firing at each other. Will Scott tell me he likes me but Annie is jealous so he can't like me? Will he tell me he likes Annie and wants me to leave them alone? I'm not looking forward to any of the answers, now that we are here together.

"A woman is pursuing my father," he says in a tight voice.

An involuntary sigh of relief escapes me when I understand that his worries don't concern me.

"You heard me?" he says, clenching his jaw.

"I did. What do you mean?"

Scott takes a deep breath. "Isn't it clear enough? That woman just doesn't leave my father alone."

"You know her?"

"The librarian." He bangs his fist on the floor. "I hate her!"

By now everybody in town knows that Scott's father is a recent widower. But of all people, Mademoiselle Moulin would never do anything embarrassing.

"She's not like that," I say.

"You don't know her," Scott says. "First the phone call, then the concert, now the Christmas gifts. At my door! Believe me, it's true. Can't she leave us alone?"

Although I was at first relieved that Scott's concerns are none of my business, I feel like my world is crumbling, too. If Scott is right, then can I trust anyone? I think of Mademoiselle Moulin sorting records for me, talking about Ibrahim and the immigrants, and being so excited about Scott moving here. She can't be the one he's describing. But I have to admit that adults can be deceiving.

"That's terrible," I say, taking my mittens off and reaching for Scott's hand.

30 AN AMERICAN PICNIC

[Scott, February 9, 1971:]

Not matter how hard we tried, our Christmas tree looks puny and our gifts are poorly wrapped. I don't even know if the librarian has picked some of them. On Christmas day, Dad made a big deal of adding chestnuts around the turkey like the French do, and he even bought the special cake shaped like a Yule log. It's called a bûche de Noël and it's decorated with miniature plastic pine trees or pine branches, mushrooms made of meringue, and other winter stuff. Back home, we had ham and Mom baked cookies that we ate with different kinds of puddings. So much better than this French menu.

Stacey poked through her plate without appetite, reminding us that we need more than food to forget how much we miss Mom. Anyway, with the American troops' deaths in Vietnam rising to forty-four thousand, Mom would have wanted a lean

Christmas.

The New Year came, and although Troubadour invited us and made sure we had good music and food, I kept thinking that there was no reason why 1971 would be better than 1970. Troubadour invited us again for the celebration of Epiphany. Stacey found the small porcelain figurine that's hidden in a special cake that tastes like almonds and butter, and she was crowned queen for the day. She had pity on me and picked me as her king.

Brigitte went to Paris over winter break and came back to school with a wardrobe worthy of a Hollywood star.

Ibrahim showed up in a pair of Levi's and a Hang Ten T-shirt.

"Thanks for supporting Hollywood Follies," I said.

"Great gifts," he said with a warm smile.

I didn't dare ask Sylvie where she shopped when she arrived with the exact same outfit as Ibrahim's, because she didn't seem happy to be here, and besides I remembered her grandmother's shopping spree at the store.

Dad made crepes for the festival of la Chandeleur, but the batter was so runny he couldn't flip one single crepe, so we ended up eating pasta for the fourth time that week. I suppose my classic cookbook wasn't such a great gift after all.

I hid my Valentines just in time. In France, only the adults celebrate with red roses and a dinner. We stayed home, reading the sweet Valentines Stacey made for us.

Days go by, so much alike that sometimes I forget if it is a Tuesday or Thursday. It snows and rains, and only my guitar brings some kind of light through the dark tunnel of my life. Sylvie said it was terrible when I told her about my dad and the librarian, but I wonder if she thinks I am making a big deal out of nothing. Anyway, in retaliation, I quit going to the library. Since the weather has been awful, I haven't seen Sylvie since Christmas Day. Lousy. It's not like me to be a whiner, and I hate it.

When I wake up today, it isn't raining, and I'm immediately in a better mood. I remember I owe Sylvie an American picnic, so I prepare a couple of sandwiches with sliced bread, ham, and camembert instead of orange American cheese. On my way to school, I buy a bag of potato chips and a bottle of Coca-Cola, which I stick in my bag.

During class, I'm thinking of my strategy for inviting Sylvie to la cabane when Brigitte elbows me. I jump, lost in my picnic's thoughts. Brigitte points toward the blackboard with her chin.

Monsieur Leroy has written: "Scott Sweet should consider boarding the next Apollo spacecraft, since he is already living in outer space." Everybody cracks up.

"The winter can be soporific here," he says. "I bet you miss the sun."

You have no idea how much more than the sun I miss. But I don't feel like sharing that, and I smile. "Spring will come, right?" I say.

"I appreciate your optimism." Monsieur Leroy puts his chalk away. "Besides you're right. Spring will be here before we know it, which brings us to your peace rally. Any news?"

Every head turns toward me once more. I feel ashamed when I realize that my personal life has sucked out all of my energy. I have become a softie preoccupied by people's opinions, my father's personal life, and girls. What a shame, while the world is bleeding and needs every ounce of energy to fight against the war!

I clear my throat. "I hope more people have considered helping." But at a glance, I see that no new names have been added to the volunteers' sign up sheet.

"It's only February," Monsieur Leroy says in a cheerful tone. "We still have time until May."

"Monsieur! Monsieur!" Brigitte's hand is stretched toward the ceiling.

"Yes, Brigitte?"

She jumps to her feet. "I'm throwing a party for Mardi Gras."

"Very nice, Brigitte," Monsieur Leroy says. "Now, would you sit down?"

"Actually," she goes on. "The whole class is invited!"

"*Oui! Chouette!*" Everybody is up, cheering at the news.

"Costumed!" Brigitte says. "And you are invited,

too, Monsieur."

"I'm afraid I can't." He pats his stomach. "My wife makes mean apple beignets for Mardi Gras. I would start a war if I celebrated elsewhere. And we don't need more violence, do we?"

Thanks to Brigitte, the rest of the day zooms away with talk of Mardi Gras costumes. The second good news of the day is that the sun is still out when we leave school.

I catch Sylvie as she passes by. "Want to go to la cabane?"

"I have to walk Elle home first," she says.

"Let's drop the girls at the store. It'll give us more time."

She frowns, considering my offer. "I can't. I didn't ask for permission."

I make a quick, reassuring mental checklist: I'm not wearing my most radical jacket today, my hair is combed, and my feet are clean.

"I'll go with you and we can ask your mother."

Sylvie chews on her lip, hesitating. "Okay," she says. "I'll tell her that I'm helping you with a French book."

We drop Stacey at the store, and I follow Sylvie and Elle through downtown Château Moines, and then up a short shaded street. We hear a dog's happy barking, and Elle gallops ahead of us.

"Chocolat!" she calls. "I'm home!"

We reach a white house that stands in the middle of a fenced yard. Sylvie's mother is standing at the gate. She waves a postcard in the air when she sees us.

"Your father wrote," she says.

"Papa!" Elle says. "You hear that, Sylvie? And you, Chocolat?" She pets the dog, who barks once and hands her his paw.

"He'll be home on Saturday," Sylvie's mother says. "I baked an apple pie to celebrate the good news."

"Maman," Sylvie says. "This is Scott. He's in my class. He moved from—"

"I know who he is." She takes in my outfit with a quick glance. "Do you like pie?"

I'm thinking that by the time we're done eating it will be dark. But I know it's rude to refuse an invitation. "I love pie, Madame Pottier," I say in my most polite voice and most perfect French. "But since it isn't raining today, we were hoping to do our homework in the park."

"Don't you love his accent?" Elle says, beaming at me.

Her mother ignores Elle and searches my eyes. "I'm glad you focus on your homework and have given up on this peace rally Sylvie told us about."

"We didn't give—" I start, but Sylvie silences me with a widening of her eyes and I nod. A nod isn't like a promise, right?

It must pass for one, because Sylvie's mother says, "Let me pack two slices of pie."

"*Merci*, Madame," I say.

"Can I go see Stacey, Maman?" Elle asks, when her mother has returned inside.

193

"It's getting late, Elle, you stay home."

"Not fair!" Elle says. "Then, can I go with Sylvie and Scott?"

"No way," Sylvie says.

"Where are you going? What are you doing?" Elle insists.

"None of your business," Sylvie says.

Elle makes a face and we laugh. Sylvie grabs the bag her mother has prepared and we take off, followed by Chocolat, but not before I catch Elle glaring furiously at her sister.

31 A PINK MERINGUE

[*Sylvie:*]

W hat's up with giving up the peace rally?" Scott says, as soon as we are on the street. "Did you chicken out?"

"I already told you to stop calling me a chicken," I say. "I never said I wouldn't do the rally, but I never really said anything to my parents about it either." I still remember their reaction the day the subject came up.

"You haven't told them?" Scott shakes his head. "I can't believe it!"

"Easy for you," I say. "You can do whatever you want. Your father is a hippie."

Scott nudges my side. "Sorry, but you haven't really seen any hippies. And for your information, my dad is still a father, and I have to ask for permission."

"When my father is home, I'll tell them." I push this conversation to the back of my mind, although it's getting crowded in there.

"Your father's away a lot," Scott says. "I suppose that's hard."

"My mother and Elle freak out when he doesn't call every other day."

I don't tell Scott that I worry, too. If anything happens to my father this time, I'll have to live with the regret of not having been able to tell him about the peace rally and my plans for my future, even though they might not please him.

Yesterday evening, I wrote until my hand cramped and I heard the clock strike eleven o'clock. But when I switched the light off, I felt restless. I hadn't been able to find any good lyrics to capture my mood or a good slogan for the peace rally. Tangled in my sheets, I grabbed the flashlight I keep under my bed and read again and again some of the words I wrote earlier. Even if I hum they sound terrible.

Look at me and see through me.
The person I am is a foreigner to you.
I'm so much more than a small-town girl.

Yuck! I thought. Panic kept me awake for another hour. What if I my singing and songwriting are so bad I could never make it to Paris? What if I was forever stuck in Château Moines? What if May 8th arrives and I haven't come up with anything? I threw my pillow over my head to shut out my freaky questions.

Scott's right, it's hard to have a father away so much, but now that he'll be home, I'll get another chance at making things better, my inspiration will return, and I'll ask permission to march against the

Vietnam War. So as we walk to la cabane I feel like I've grown wings. Chocolat is happy, too, and his paws spatter and splatter through the mud.

"At least," Scott says, interrupting my thoughts, "Your father returns. My mother won't ever come back."

This is the first time Scott tells me anything directly about his mother.

"Someday, you'll get to be with her," I say in a soft voice, as if I was tiptoeing to his heart.

His laugh is like a cut on my skin. "I became an agnostic," he says.

"You don't believe in God?"

"I didn't say *atheist*. I just think that it's impossible to know whether or not God exists." Scott chuckles. "Really, what kind of god would let the world get so violent?"

Chocolat sits between us, unmindful of the mud. He offers his paw to Scott, as if he knew that small comforts are better than big speeches. Scott shakes it, but doesn't smile or say anything. Chocolat cocks his head with concern. I wish I had my notebook to unload my own worries.

First there was the war,
Then the peace rally,
Now the religion.
Ibrahim believes in Allah.
I believe in God.
What for the agnostics?

"So?" Scott says. "What do you think?"

197

"I don't know," I say with a shrug.

Scott's real smile heals the cut his laughter made. "Me neither," he says. He digs into his pocket and opens his hand. The earring I saw months ago shines in his palm. "The only thing I know," he says. "Is that my mom wore these earrings. Period."

I'd like to be as bold as I was the day Scott told me about Mademoiselle Moulin and his father, but I think I will only upset him if I say I understand. Words can hurt more than silence, so I remain quiet. I could take his hand, but I'm not sure of Scott's feelings for me, so I stuff my hands in my pockets. Even Chocolat knows better than to bark when a bird flies low above our heads. The sound of my boots, of Scott's sandals, and Chocolat's paws splashing through the slushy ground accompany us to la cabane.

Scott turns the knob and the door opens. "Funny. I'd swear I locked it."

Chocolat bounds inside. Piece by piece, I take in Scott's music and the candles on the table, the pillows left in a heap, and the blankets folded on a chair.

"Everything looks okay," I say, swatting at a cobweb. "Just needs some cleanup."

Scott digs through his bag and hands me a sandwich. "I promised you an American picnic," he says. He tears a bag of potato chips open and offers me the bag.

"Thanks." I sit on one of the pillows and Scott joins me.

We pass the bottle of Coca-Cola between us as we shove our hands into the bag of chips.

"Your sandwiches are good," I say, my mouth full.

"Too bad I couldn't find any Wonder Bread," Scott says, with an apologetic shrug.

We attack the slices of pie, with Chocolat pacing between us, begging for a piece or at least a crumb. Suddenly oblivious to us, he sniffs the ground, sticks his nose in a corner, and doesn't budge.

"What is he doing?" Scott says.

"What is it, Chocolat?" But he ignores me, munching with voracity. I jump to my feet and have to use both of my hands to pry his mouth open.

"What's that?" Scott asks, when I retrieve a pink gooey thing dripping with saliva.

"A meringue." I dangle it between my fingers. Chocolat stretches out his neck. "Don't!" I shout, but he snatches the meringue, which disappears with a slurp in his slobbering mouth.

"Is it that good?" Scott says. "I've never had one."

"I hate meringues, but it's my sister's favorite cookie."

"Do you think Elle …?" Scott says.

I shake my head. "She would never come here alone." I wipe my sticky hands on my pants, pausing for a dramatic effect. "But meringues are made at the Duvals' bakery."

Scott opens his mouth, but I don't let him talk.

"It can only be Annie," I say.

32   SOCCER GAME OR COSTUME PARTY?

[*Scott, February 23, 1971:*]

"Can you play it again? Please!" Stacey joins her hands prayer-like.

"No." Yet I strum my guitar just to watch her eyes grow wide with admiration.

Using the small change Dad let me have from grocery shopping, I've bought three new songbooks for guitar since the fall. The thick calluses at the tips of my fingers on my left hand, and the long fingernails on my right hand prove to me that I'm getting there. Troubadour says I passed the intermediate level and could reach the advanced one if I took lessons. If only business wasn't so slow!

The weather is too cold for the spring clothes that Dad got from L.A. Now the boutique is packed with a mix of winter and summer clothing and too many knick-knacks, which take up all of the space. And I'm thinking that my brain is like Hollywood Follies, crowded with many disorganized thoughts, keeping me restless.

First of all, now that I've welcomed everybody on board the peace rally boat, I must go on. They believe I'm an expert, but I have a lot to do before May 8th.

Second of all, since Chocolat ate the meringue or whatever French cookie it was, Sylvie is 100% positive Annie entered la cabane. Meaning, Sylvie says, that she saw la cabane the day we found it and knows we meet there. Still according to Sylvie, Annie is a hypocrite, since she accepted Sylvie's Christmas gift and offered her one as well. Personally, I don't believe Annie would have been able to keep this information to herself. She would have exploded already.

To add to my thoughts, there is Brigitte's Mardi Gras party. Today.

I can't believe I said yes. *This is your first French party*, I keep telling myself, *and you can't flunk it.* The real reason I'm nervous is that it is my first party. Ever. Pete and Mike would be in shock if they knew a girl invited me to a party and that I'm going.

"Come on!" Stacey's cheerful clapping brings me back to planet earth. "Play a song for me!"

I put my guitar down. "I've got to get ready."

"Where are you going?" Stacey puts her hands on her hips.

"A party," I say, as if I were a pro on parties.

"A party? You didn't tell me! Come on, let me help you."

And before I can say a word, my sister is in my closet, going through my shirts, inspecting them, discarding most, and selecting a few. "Let me see," she says as she matches the shirts to my jeans. Since all of my jeans look the same except for the fading, it leaves few options. Now Stacey digs through my drawer and pulls out my scarves. She works in silence, frowning and chewing on her bottom lip. "Voilà!" she says, with her Mom's grin.

I check the outfit that lies on my bed: a pair of bell-bottom jeans, an Indian shirt, the Palestinian headscarf Ibrahim gave me, and a pair of platform shoes Stacey no doubt found downstairs in the store.

"Nah," I say, pointing at the shoes. "No socks until the end of the war."

"You can be barefoot inside."

I shake my head no. "Doesn't count that way."

Stacey sighs. "You are ruining the outfit, but whatever." She trades the platform shoes for a pair of Indian sandals and adds a necklace with a peace sign.

"Now," I say, "get out or I'll change right in front of you!"

"Ugh!" She runs away, screaming and giggling at the same time.

When I'm dressed, I choose a few records from my favorites, just in case there is only French music.

Brigitte's house is within roller-skating distance from downtown, but when I reach her street, lined with tall trees, I feel like I'm in another town. A large woodsy park surrounds each house, and fancy cars are parked along the graveled alleys. Even the sidewalks are wider. I check Brigitte's address and see Ibrahim leaning against the gate.

"Cool costume," I say, taking in his soccer shorts and jersey. He even wears his muddy cleats and has a soccer ball is stuck under his arm.

"This is no costume," he says. "I'm not going."

"Why not? Parties are fun," I say, party expert that I am. "Food! Music! Dance!" I lean towards him. "And the best part: girls!"

I swear Ibrahim nearly rolls his eyes. "I'm still not going."

"So why are you here?" I take off my roller skates.

"To invite you to my game."

"Thanks. Of course, I'll go. When is it?"

"Today. During the party," Ibrahim says.

"I don't think I can make it. That's too bad."

"Me or the party."

"Excuse me?" I laugh at the tone of Ibrahim's voice and also at the fact that he's making me choose like that, right in front of Brigitte's mansion. Brigitte, by the way, is now standing on the front steps and welcoming everyone. "Come on," I say. "Brigitte is pretty cool to invite everybody. You included, by the way."

"Are you asking me to cancel my game?" Ibrahim drums his fingers on the ball.

I throw my hands in the air. "How can you ask me to choose? I said yes to Brigitte before I knew you had a game."

"Are you coming or not?" He drums faster.

"I've never missed one of your games anyway."

"Got it." Ibrahim's halfway down the street when he turns back. "You're nothing like your father," he shouts. "He sticks to his beliefs." And he takes off.

"Scott! Come on!" It's Brigitte, calling from her doorsteps.

"Coming!" I shout back, but my eyes follow the red-and-black soccer outfit until it disappears around the corner of the street.

What does Ibrahim mean about my father? It's not like he knows him. He saw him a couple of times, but that's it. What could he know about Dad that I don't know? I have to take a couple of deep breaths to calm down before following a group of kids inside Brigitte's castle.

33 MARDI GRAS SPOILERS

[*Sylvie, February 23, 1971:*]

Brigitte is waving a purple feather boa that matches her lipstick, to show us the way to the basement. The long winding stairway is alight with tiny paper lanterns. I'm careful not to step on my long dress as I follow the sound of "Gimme Shelter" playing full blast. I think Brigitte is lucky that her parents let her play loud music.

"Sorry," I say when I bump into a girl walking down the stairs just ahead of me.

The girl peeks over her shoulder. It's Annie. A quick smile curls her lips up. "Great costume," she says.

At a glance, I realize we are wearing identical gypsy dresses. "Yours isn't bad either," I say.

"Made out of scraps I found at home," she tells me when we get downstairs.

"Same here."

She points at my large golden pair of earrings.

"Where did you get that?"

"I made them. Easy: two jar lids that I taped on my earlobes."

"Clever."

We sit next to each other on one of the four plush sofas arranged in a big square. We give the appearance of being friends again, but we both know something has changed. Like when you miss the beginning of a movie on TV and you would like to rewind it but you can't. Our friendship can't go back to where it was before Scott arrived; it can only move forward.

"I'm glad you came," I say.

"I suppose I am, too," Annie says, just as Scott appears at the bottom of the stairs.

A bunch of records are stacked under his arm, and although he looks the same in his ragged jeans, his army jacket, and his sandals, he seems preoccupied and unaware of the people dancing and laughing all over the basement.

"Scott!" Brigitte says. "I said *costumed*!"

"Ask my sister," he says, heading straight for the record player.

The words I'd like to tell him form in my head.

I'd like to run to you,
Ask you
What's wrong with you?
Tell you
That your sadness breaks my heart
And ask you to

Share your sorrow with me.

Annie ogles the cookies and the pitcher of lemonade. "I'm hungry," she says standing up.

"I'll stay."

Scott browses through the pile of records until he picks "Black Magic Woman" from his own records. Brigitte switches off some lights. Most of my classmates start to dance.

"Want some?" Annie hands me a plate with an assortment of cookies.

A pink meringue sits in the middle. I pick it up and I turn it between my fingers. "Are the meringues sold in Château Moines only made at your bakery?" I ask.

"I believe so," Annie says. "Why?"

"For no reason. The other day Chocolat found one and ate it whole."

Annie explodes in laughter. "I had no idea a dog would like meringues. But I know that you don't." I hand her the meringue, which she gobbles on her way to the dance floor.

Did she drop a meringue at la cabane or not? Is she a great liar, or is she innocent?

Scott's voice takes me away from my speculations. He takes in my gypsy dress and earrings. "Cool costume," he says.

"Thanks." I make room for him.

He smells of his usual mix of patchouli and shampoo, a smell that I've come to recognize without even thinking. He's quiet, but it's perfect with me. We just sit next to each other, watching our entire class dance. Someone has cranked the volume up. The disco balls flash, and since everyone is costumed, it's hard to know who is who. Scott's funny guesses make me laugh.

"Is that Brigitte dancing?" He points at a couple.

The girl wears a feather boa and high heels. "Definitely Brigitte," I say. "But the boy? No clue. You know what? It's cool that everyone came."

"Everyone didn't come." Scott's voice doesn't hide his disappointment.

"I think we are all here," I say, straining my eyes. "Wait, where is Ibrahim?"

"Told you."

"Maybe he wasn't allowed." I catch Scott's glare. "You know, being from another country. I mean religion and everything."

"Has nothing to do with him being Muslim." Scott taps his foot to the beat of the music. "Right now, he's playing soccer."

"He only plays at school."

"You don't believe me?"

"Look, there is one soccer field in town, and the Arabs don't use it."

"That figures," Scott says.

"They kept fighting." I realize how stupid and unfair the idea is, since nobody knows who started the fight. In the end the Arabs gave up the field. "So, where is he playing?"

"You don't want to know." He stands up and offers me his hand. "You dance?"

I've never danced with a boy in my entire life. In a flash, my heart morphs into a bird trapped inside a cage. Panicked, the bird flutters his wings to escape. Scott and I stand at least thirty centimeters away from each other.

"Can someone put on "Bridge Over Trouble Water," please?" he calls.

As soon as the guitars, harmonicas, and voices of Simon and Garfunkel fill the basement, he wraps his arms around my waist, and I bring mine to his neck, as if I knew what to do. I watch my step so I won't crush his sandaled feet. We aren't really dancing, so it's easy. I'm starting to get the hang of it when Brigitte waves her arms up in the air like an octopus.

"My parents! My parents are home!" She switches the disco balls off.

Scott is the fastest to reach for the record player. But he's still holding onto my waist, and I trip on the long hem of my dress. He catches me just before I fall flat on the ground and drags me to my feet. When I'm up, our faces are so close to each other that I can almost taste the gum he has been chewing.

"It was my first slow dance with a girl," he says, his breath sweet and light in my ear. At the same second, someone turns the lights on.

"What's going on in here?" A man's voice booms through the basement. He loosens his tie as if he couldn't breathe and drops a small suitcase on the ground.

"I'll clean up, Papa," Brigitte says, stepping

forward.

A woman in an elegant suit stands next to Brigitte's father.

"Clean up?" she says in a drained voice. "As if cleaning up would change the fact that while we were on the road you've been talked into this silly ..." She takes in the food and the pillows on the floor, the costumes and masks in a weary glance.

"I'm sorry, Maman," Brigitte says, twisting her feather boa. "But nobody talked me into anything. I had the idea. Alone."

"Even better," her father says. "Do you think we need more drama to spice our lives?"

"It's Mardi Gras," Brigitte says. "I wanted to have fun."

Her father flings his arms wide open. "While your parents worry with so many problems?"

"I never get to do anything," Brigitte says, holding his stare.

Words collide inside my head, and I realize that life is rarely what it looks like.

34 WALKING IN EACH OTHER'S SHOES

[*Scott:*]

I can't believe I told Sylvie about Ibrahim's game. On top of it, she told Annie, who said she would love to watch Ibrahim play. I'm dreading this game thing. Now we are the only light-skinned kids who crowd around the muddy field where Ibrahim plays, but we cheer with the same enthusiasm as the others. The two teams are made of boys who live in the projects. All are terrific players, although Ibrahim is by far the best.

"He's sooo good!" Annie claps her hands each time Ibrahim shoots a goal.

I'm relieved that he hasn't seen any of us yet. "If he played on a real field instead of this piece of dirt," I say, "he'd be a star."

Sylvie keeps her eyes on the hem of her dress, now caked with mud. "Told you," she says. "They don't get along, the French and the Arabs."

"It's such a waste," I say. "Château Moines would win every single game with Ibrahim on the town's team."

"Hey," Annie says. "You're preaching to the choir."

"I had no idea they played here," Sylvie says. "I suppose nobody knows."

"Nobody wants to know," Annie says, cheering at Ibrahim's next goal.

After the game, Ibrahim spots us. He narrows his eyes, wipes his sweaty face with his jersey, and marches toward me. He juts his chin toward Sylvie and Annie. "What are they doing here? You promised."

"They love soccer." I lower my voice. "Annie's a real fan of yours."

Ibrahim nudges me with his elbow. "The party was so boring?"

"For your information, I left a groovy party for a lousy soccer game."

"Consider your visit a privilege," Ibrahim tells the girls. He jogs toward a shabby shed. Halfway, he turns around. "Wait for me. You'll buy me a drink at the café."

"They don't have a field, but they must have a good coach," Sylvie says, as we watch the boys walk to the makeshift changing room.

"Are you kidding?" I say. "They coach themselves."

"Pathetic," Annie says. She waves at Ibrahim, who

has changed into the pair of Levi's he hasn't stopped wearing since Christmas.

We walk to Chez Lili, talking about the game, the party, and Brigitte's parents.

"I get it," Ibrahim says. "The party went kaput so you came to see me."

"Oh, please!" I tell him as we enter the café.

Garçon nods from the counter and prepares four diabolo menthes, which he brings to my regular table. Sylvie sits next to me and Ibrahim and Annie sit across from us.

"What's up with Brigitte's parents, anyway?" Ibrahim says, toying with a straw.

"They seemed pretty pissed off," I say.

"She hadn't told them about the party," Annie says.

"My parents would throw a fit, too," Sylvie says.

Annie chuckles. "That's the good part of not having any."

"Huh," Ibrahim says. "Parties are family stuff at my home."

"Couscous night sounds like fun," I say.

"I suppose." Ibrahim twirls the straw in his glass. "Suffocating, too."

I think of his large family, sharing weekly couscous nights together, and of our big empty apartment and our pasta dinners. "Suffocating isn't that bad," I say.

"You don't know what a big family is." Ibrahim polishes off his glass with a large gulp.

"No comment," Annie says.

Next to me, Sylvie keeps silent, and I wonder if this is how she gets inspiration for her songs. Observing how people get messed up with their complicated lives can be a pretty good source, I suppose, but somehow it annoys me that she chooses to be quiet rather than sharing her thoughts with us. I drum my fingers against my glass.

"Sylvie, what do you think?" I ask.

I've jolted her and she blinks. "What?" she says, and I regret my tone of voice.

"Is your family suffocating, too?"

"That's what families are supposed to be, right? Do you know of any who aren't?"

Ibrahim smiles; he must think that Sylvie caught me in my own trap.

"You know what?" I say. "I think you guys have it real good without appreciating it."

"Hello?" Annie says. "You still have a father and a sister."

"Listen," Ibrahim says. He brings his hands flat on the table. "We should walk in each other's shoes before making judgments."

"Then," Sylvie says with a gentle tap on my arm. "I'll wait for summer, if I have to walk without socks in Scott's weird sandals."

We all crack up, and I nearly strangle myself when the librarian walks through the door. She sets her macramé bag on the counter.

"I've got to go," I say.

"Me, too." Ibrahim stands up. "You girls are

coming?"

I tag along, hoping the librarian won't pay attention to a bunch of kids. But when we pass her, she turns sideways to get something from her bag. A smile breaks across her face.

"Great costumes," she says, admiring Annie and Sylvie.

"We went to a party," Sylvie says.

"Then," Annie says, "we watched Ibrahim's game. He scored the most goals."

"I heard your team is getting better and better," the librarian says.

"They would be better and better if they played on a decent field," Annie says. "Why isn't the Centre d'Assimilation pour Immigrants doing something?"

"Point taken." The librarian sips some of her coffee. "A committee is now addressing the budgets issues."

"Huh," I say. "We really should be going."

"Also, Ibrahim," she says, "the center is hoping," and she crosses her fingers, "to make a second round of distributions this summer."

"That would be *chouette*," Ibrahim says.

"I need to talk with concerned business owners," she says with a definite smile in my direction. "We have to get more involvement."

"Woah! I'm late!" I say. I rush to the door.

Sylvie, Ibrahim, and Annie catch up with me in the street.

"What's up with you?" Annie says.

"Scott has his reasons," Sylvie says. "People aren't always what they seem to be."

Ibrahim looks alternatively at Sylvie and me. "Mademoiselle Moulin looks okay to me. She's fair. Plus, you heard her? She says she wants more business support. That would be good publicity for your father, right?"

"The other way around would be better. More support *for* business owners," I say, thinking of what I could do if Dad had more customers.

Ibrahim looks at me with a puzzled look pasted on his face. "Takes time," he says with a patient sigh. "Support can only come slowly."

"I suppose," I say, and Sylvie and Annie nod in agreement.

35 GIVE PEACE A CHANCE

[Sylvie, April 24, 1971:]

Papa wipes his mouth. "Simone, you're a real chef!"

"It's a basic veal stew," Maman says, but she blushes.

"Can I have more?" Elle hands her plate across and Maman spoons half a ladle.

"Ah!" Papa sighs, when the only sound in the kitchen comes from the clinking of our forks and knifes. "What is better than being home and sharing a good meal with your family? The rest of the world could collapse; we wouldn't even notice."

I shoot him a quick glance. Now that every cell of my brain is filled with ideas for a slogan for the peace march, Papa's personal view on peace seems a little narrow.

I set my knife on the table. "I'm finished." I catch Maman's eye on my half-full plate. The phone saves me. "I'll get it."

On the other end of the line, Scott is breathless. "Have you watched the news? John Denver sang "The Strangest Dream" and Peter, Paul, and Mary sang—"

"Scott," I say. "Can you speak in French?"

"Oh, sorry," he says in English before switching to French. "I'm so excited! Five hundred thousand people gathered in Washington, DC, for a peace march. Sylvie, I can't wait for our own rally!"

"Me neither," I say, although a nervous bird flaps his wings in my ribcage whenever I think of the slogan I haven't found yet.

"Who is it?" Papa calls from the kitchen.

"Coming!"

"Watch the news," Scott says. "See you at la cabane tomorrow." He hangs up with a victorious: "Peace on earth!"

"Switch the TV on!" I shout.

"What's going on?" Papa balls up his napkin.

"The news!"

We all hurry to La Boutique. Maman drapes the new dress she is sewing on the back of a chair and we squeeze onto the sofa. A sea of bodies fills the TV screen.

Elle's eyes are as wide as the crowd. "Is it Santa Monica?" she says. "Is it where Stacey lived before?"

Papa takes her small hand in his. "This is Washington DC, the capital of the USA," he says. "Stacey lived in California."

"Good," Elle says. "There are too many people in

this town."

Three musicians, a woman with long blond hair and two men with mustaches and guitars, are singing on a stage, while people all over the plaza are waving huge homemade peace signs. The camera travels through the dense crowd, and I keep my eyes wide open on the men with long hair and beards and the women in long dresses or jeans. They hold hands as they sway to the sound of the guitars. Many sit on the ground, while others are perched on statues and fountains or stroll among the people.

I don't understand the words of the song, but everyone is singing with the musicians, and the humming flows from the stage to my home, thousands of kilometers away. I glance at my family, wondering if, like me, despite the distance, they feel connected to this crowd, powerless on this bloody planet earth, yet hopeful that together we can stop a war.

"What are they doing?" Elle asks. "What are they saying? Who are the singers?"

Maman stands up. "They live very far from us, and we haven't had our dessert."

But Elle doesn't move. "I want to know what they are doing."

"They want to stop the war in Vietnam," I say.

A big smile illumines Elle's face. "Just like you," she says.

"What do you mean?" Maman says.

"The big kids are also doing a peace march," Elle

says. "Right, Sylvie?"

"I thought you canceled." Maman looks straight into my eyes.

"Oh, non!" Elle says before I can open my mouth. "They are doing it."

Maman turns the TV off. "I already gave you my opinion, Sylvie. Be at peace here before marching against a war the French people aren't even involved in."

I reach for her arm. "Maman, everybody is involved."

She stiffens. "It's not like sitting on the ground, playing the guitar, and singing will bring peace."

"And what will?"

Elle shifts her stare from Maman to me as if she was watching a Ping-pong game.

"These are too serious topics for young girls like you." Papa wraps his arm around Maman's shoulders. "You'll deal with problems soon enough. Let's eat dessert!"

Maman lifts her eyes to meet Papa's. "You're right. We can't change the world just like that." She snaps her fingers. "Peace starts here." And she leads us to the kitchen.

I'm boiling inside, and I can't hold the lid on my angry pot anymore. "How can you eat dessert, even think of dessert, when people are dying in Vietnam?"

Maman sets the dessert plates down without a word or a glance in my direction. Elle is looking alternatively at me and at Papa and Maman, searching for clues, but in the end she slides into her chair. Papa scratches his head and takes a seat, too. Chocolat, seeing everyone seated, believes everything is normal again and lies down at my feet.

But I can't pretend everything is normal. I just can't lie and fake it anymore. I ball up my napkin, throw it on the floor, and stampede away.

"I said peace starts at home," Maman says.

I pivot, ready to explode again, but the mist I catch in her eyes stops me.

"Come on," Elle says, in such a small voice that I can't ignore her. "Tell us about the peace march."

"Maybe later," I say. "There is something I need to finish first."

Papa nods. "Go then," he says.

"Pies are better when they have cooled off a bit, anyway," Maman says.

I climb the stairs, thinking that if peace is so hard to reach at home with pies, no wonder there is war all over the world.

My notebook waits for me, nestled in my trunk. The 500,000 peace protesters on TV, my parents' indifference, and yet their change of heart bring mixed words to my blank page.

Indifference Kills Peace. Peace Has No Borders. Together to Heal Bloody Earth. Divided We Create Discord. As One We Build Peace. Peaceful Us Stop Violent Us. Give Peace a Chance.

None is a good slogan, though. What if I can't find any? Panic makes my stomach hurt. I chew on my pencil, unable to find better words, and then I realize that three synonyms of the word "together" are musical words: in sync, in harmony, and in concert. I write them down, hoping they will inspire me, and I tuck my notebook away.

36 BLOWING IN THE WIND

[*Scott:*]

Dad switched the TV off a long time ago, but the images of the people climbing the statues all over the Mall in Washington, DC, are still playing behind my eyes. I feel restless and, although it's dark outside, I grab my jacket and go to the door.

"Mind if I join you?" Dad says.

Back home, Mom took us for a walk around the block every night. If Dad wants a walk, he'll get one. But he'd better be ready for questions and answers. I want the librarian out of our lives, one way or another. Tonight looks like the perfect time.

"What about Stacey?" I say.

"I'll go check on her." Dad returns with his denim jacket on. "She rolled her eyes and said she doesn't need two full-time babysitters."

I cannot believe how quiet Château Moines is, while half a million people gathered today in DC to protest the Vietnam War. It worries me when I think that in less than two weeks, we will be also protesting the war. Will anyone show up?

"Something on your mind?" Dad asks.

I shrug one shoulder. "Not really." Now that his arm brushes against mine, it's hard to dump my load of embarrassing questions on him.

Our footsteps resonate along rue Principale. The street looks like one of those historical replica towns we have in America. The bakery's window is bare, and I wonder where the cakes go for the night. The metallic flower containers, which stand in front of the shop during the day, are also gone. Only Chez Lili seems alive at the corner of the street.

"Thirsty?" Dad says, feeling his pockets for some change.

The lights have been dimmed inside the café and the music is playing low. A handful of customers lean over the counter.

Garçon juts his chin out to say hello when he sees us coming in. I jut my chin back.

"I see," Dad says, following me to the window booth, "you're a true habitué."

"This is my father," I tell Garçon when he sets two diabolo menthes on the table.

"*Enchanté.* They call me Garçon." He shakes Dad's hand. "A good boy you have here."

It brings an immediate smile on Dad's face and a stupid look on mine. *Why does Garçon make fun of me if he thinks I'm a good boy? Is it another French thing?*

"This peace rally he's planning," he says. "He's been working hard at it." He makes the peace sign. "He's far out," he adds in English. I swallow my drink the wrong way and Garçon brings his palms up. "I won't ever speak English without warning you."

Dad sips his drink, an amused smile on his lips. Garçon lowers his eyes. "Not easy to raise kids alone. You're doing a fine job." He steps back to the counter.

Dad doesn't move for a few seconds. "I'll be right back," he says. I watch him as he slips a franc in the jukebox and selects a song.

The first notes of "Blowin' in the Wind" and then the voices of Peter, Paul, and Mary fill the café. Dad returns to the booth. Does he, like me, feels displaced tonight? Does he feel we are spoiled and don't deserve to be in this peaceful town, miles away from the turmoil of America? Does he also feel kind of sad, now that our voices don't count anymore? He doesn't say anything, and my thoughts go on and on until the song ends.

"Do you remember?" Dad says and his voice makes me jump. "When Bob Dylan released this song in 1963?"

"Dad, I was a baby back then." I twirl the straw in my glass.

Dad slaps his forehead. I wonder if, for the time of the song, he had forgotten about me and thought he was talking to Mom.

"It's a great song, anyway," I say. I forget about

the librarian and instead feel like fitting Garçon's definition and being the nicest son on earth. However, the song takes my mind back to the protest. "Dad, do you think I should cancel the peace rally?"

"And why would you do that?" he says, raising his eyebrows in concern.

I shrug. "Not sure this is the right place for a protest."

"You forget how the French love protests." He leans into me. "I guarantee you, they will come. Walking the streets with banners and chanting some kind of slogan makes any French person feel alive."

Sylvie was passionate when she spoke about May 1968 and the barricades. Dad's right: The French are good at protesting.

"Still," I say, "do you think they will support something that comes from an American kid? Protesting an American war?"

"You've got a point. The war isn't a top priority now that they've left Vietnam."

"So I should give up?"

"You've involved your new friends in this project." Dad polishes off his drink. "You can't just step away because you're a little afraid. Even if it turns out to be a flop, you have to do it."

Once in a while the beams of a car slice the window and illuminate Dad's face. He has lost his California tan, and new wrinkles web his eyes.

"I'll do it," I say, feeling selfish and also like a wet hen.

Dad brings his hand to my arm. "The man's right," he says in a soft voice. "You're a good boy."

Someone puts some money in the jukebox and a French popular song reaches us.

"Ah," Dad says with a sigh. "French music! Another thing they do differently than us."

"Better?" I ask. Now that he has told me about the French talent for street demonstrations, I think of Sylvie writing her songs.

Dad makes a funny face. "I said different, Scott." He cups his hand around his mouth. "Better cooks than musicians if you want my opinion, but somehow their songs are beautiful."

We listen to the French song, which neither Dad nor I can sing right. Again, I think of Sylvie's songs and how they made my heart sing.

"Yeah," I say. "It's beautiful. Too bad Mom isn't here."

Dad has a small smile. "We wouldn't be here if she were still alive."

I of all people am aware that we agreed to a change of scenery when the sky was never blue and the ocean was always gray. "I know that, Dad."

"There is something you don't know." Dad's voice cracks a little.

He freaks me out, so I finish my drink in a gulp. "Huh, shouldn't we go home?"

But Dad doesn't answer. "When the doctors told your mom that she had less than a year to live, she got organized." He checks on me, making sure I'm all right before going on. "She listed what she had to do before …"

I squirm on my seat. I hated those months and hate to be reminded of them.

"I know it was hard on you," Dad says, squeezing his empty glass between his hands. "And your mom knew it, too. But she had to say goodbye to a few special places and make sure some paperwork was in order."

"Paperwork? When you know you are dying? I don't understand."

"Your mom was from Château Moines," Dad says.

At this exact second, I feel like a heavy coat has been thrown over my shoulders and at the same time like a window has opened onto my mother's life and mine. "What?"

"At eighteen," Dad goes on, "your mom left for Paris to pursue her studies, which was unusual for a small-town girl back then. Some locals thought she was stuck-up. When her parents died, she inherited the family store, called Le Petit Paris. Despite her dream of living in Paris, she then decided to return to Château Moines, but she had met me and instead came with me to California. She planned to sell Le Petit Paris someday. If we had added it to our savings, we would have opened a store in Santa Monica, but when your mom fell ill, we had to dig into our savings. It was too late for a store anyway. She saw an attorney and made sure I would inherit her parents' store. I promised her that Le Petit Paris would become Hollywood Follies."

"Does anyone here know you are Mom's husband?" I say. I have a hard time forgiving people for judging my mother when I know how she was anything but stuck-up.

Dad shrugs. "I haven't told anyone, but I suspect that business is slow because they are mad that she sold her parents' store to a rich American."

"Rich?" I chuckle. "Why don't you just tell them who you are?"

"It's my personal story. Besides, I want to build my clientele just by being me, and not because of some kind of pity."

"I guess I can get that," I say, thinking that in a way Mom gave us a poisoned gift. "Don't you sometimes wish that Mom hadn't asked you to come here?"

Dad folds his hands. "I promised her, Scott. I would feel terrible if I hadn't come. That's why I think you should stick to your peace rally. You also made a promise. You can't back out just because you're afraid." He opens his palms as if he is offering me something. "If you need anything, I'll be happy to help."

I think of how I wanted to confront Dad about the librarian. After what he told me, and his offer of help, I realize that he has a lot on his plate. The librarian pisses me off, but my father is here for me.

37   FINDING A SLOGAN

[*Sylvie, April 27, 1971:*]

I need the slogan," Brigitte tells me in the morning. "Now!" She drops her bag on her seat. "Otherwise, we won't have any T-shirts."

I've scribbled pages and pages of them, but nothing sounds right.

"You hear me?" Brigitte leans toward my face.

"You'll have it by 5," I say, as if I had the slightest idea how this could happen.

"Better be good," she says. "The T-shirts are state of the art." I wonder how plain white T-shirts can be state of the art. "My brother's in charge," Brigitte adds.

I ignore everyone for the rest of the day, while every cell of my brain focuses on words, more words, and only on words. By 4:30 pm I consider faking a fever and running home. I feel sweaty and dizzy anyway. When the dismissal bell rings, I hurry to the door, but Brigitte is faster. She blocks my way and tilts her head. I hand her a piece of paper folded in four. She sticks the paper in her pocket.

"You don't want to know?" I ask.

"Why? You're good at that kind of things. Besides, I like surprises."

I hope Scott likes surprises, too. I'm meeting with him at la cabane in an hour to get the final okay before they print the slogan on the T-shirts. Is Brigitte right? Scott and Annie have also called me the queen of words. Am I really good at writing?

I walk Elle home and hurry to la cabane. Scott is sitting outside, jotting notes on a pad.

"I'm done," he says when he sees me.

I drop my bag on the grass. "Me, too."

"Cool! Can I see your ideas?"

"When I say *done*, I mean really done." I pull out my pad. "Brigitte couldn't wait any longer, so I had to come up with something today." I toss my pad to Scott.

He flips page after page until he reaches the last one. He remains quiet for the longest time and my heart flip flops, unable to slow down. Scott looks up, and sparkles dance in his eyes.

"I like it," he says.

"Really?" My heart can't decide if it should calm down or not.

"'In Concert Against the War,'" he reads aloud. "I like it. Really."

It's a weird feeling to hear someone else reading

your own words.

"Also," I say. "I've got an idea."

"Yeah?" Scott waits for me to elaborate.

I've never had any real ideas, while all the time he has had so many. "We should have music. I'll ask the town band and anyone who has an instrument to play as we march."

"Cool!" Scott says. "Now we've got to make a checklist." He gets to a blank page of his pad and reads aloud as he writes:

1. Posters: Dad. Designs and prints them.

2. Banners: Dad designs. Ibrahim displays them downtown.

3. Publicity: Annie sets up the posters in every business in town.

4. T-shirts: Brigitte.

5. Security: Detective Richard and Scott.

6. Placards: Sylvie.

7. Music: Sylvie.

He flips his pad closed and gives me the high five. "That's a lot of work for you."

"I'll be fine," I say.

Winter has stepped backstage and the sun warms our skins. Like Scott, I want to believe that the peace rally is a great idea, although we won't know before the big day.

"Trust me," Scott says as we walk back to town. "Everybody will come."

I keep to myself the fact that I already know that my parents won't be there.

Instead, I give Scott my widest smile.

38 STOP THE WAR NOW!

[*Scott:*]

Dad gets to work as soon as I give him the slogan. "I like it," he says. "Can you give me a hand?"

Together we carry his art trunk up from the basement. Dad hasn't done any artwork since we opened Hollywood Follies. He examines his pencils, markers, and colored pencils. Then he slips on the pair of glasses he uses when he draws.

Stacey and I plop down around the table and watch him in silence. When we were little, Dad would give us some blank paper and watercolors, and we would paint while he worked. Tonight we observe him holding his pencil still before tracing a line. It reminds me of the few seconds before I strum my guitar. I'm never sure of the result, and it's both scary and exciting. I suppose he feels the same way.

Stacey rubs her eyes and yawns.

"Good-night, sleepyhead," Dad says, putting his pencil down.

"Please. Can I stay a little longer?"

"Ten o'clock. Way past your bedtime."

I suspect Dad will also miss his bedtime. The poster has to be finished tonight if he wants to drop it off at the print shop first thing in the morning. He shoos me away at midnight.

"I promised you I'd help," he says. "Now go to bed and sleep tight."

When I tiptoe into the living room at seven in the morning, the lights are on and the table is crowded with butcher paper, pencils, pens, and markers. Dad is curled up on the sofa, wearing yesterday's clothes. His glasses are perched on his nose. I take them off and pull the blanket up closer to his chin. He sighs but doesn't budge.

I carry a breakfast tray to Stacey's room. "It's not my birthday!" she squeals in delight.

"Hush! Dad's asleep." I pull the curtains open and pale sunlight pours into the room. We share our toast and orange juice in silence.

"You want to see the poster?" I ask Stacey when we are finished.

We stagger around a couple of empty boxes of cookies, chewing gum wrappers, cups stained with coffee, and scraps of paper, which litter the floor.

"Look!" Stacey says. She points at the coffee table.

The poster is as cool as the slogan. Dad has picked the colors red, white, and blue, which happen to be the same ones for both the French and American flags. He has painted the countryside with peace signs as a background and the silhouettes of soldiers on top of it. Some of them are falling and some of them are exploding in the air. All of them are dying. Sylvie's slogan is handwritten, and looks a little like the name of our store on the awning.

"It's perfect!" Stacey blows a kiss in direction of Dad, who hasn't moved at all, and we leave for school.

Dad forgot to check the mail yesterday and I spot a brown envelope in the mailbox. It's from Pete. He has sent me a record by Edwin Starr called "Stop the War Now!" A note falls to the ground:

Good-luck gift for the rally. Peace! Pete.

"That's nice," Stacey says, clutching my hand.

I can only agree.

The following week reminds me of the opening of Hollywood Follies. There is so much stuff to do that I have a hard time keeping up with my homework. I end up at Chez Lili most afternoons, doing my math or French homework while I get the latest updates.

Today Annie is pretty pissed off. "They say they don't want to be associated with any sort of protest," she says, explaining that several business owners have refused to display posters in their stores.

"Did you insist and tell them it's a good cause?"

"What do you think I told them?" Annie says with

a sigh. "They are stubborn." She leans toward me. "But they can't do anything if I put the posters outside their shops."

"If we want peace, we better do something peaceful."

Annie smirks. "That's noble but not practical."

"Let me talk with Troubadour and Garçon," I say. "They are also business owners, and they agreed. Maybe they can be more convincing than we are."

"I'll give it another try." Annie gathers her stack of posters, her box of tacks, and a roll of tape. "Wish me luck, peace boy."

Ibrahim pokes his head in right after Annie leaves. "Hey," he says. I look up from my math book. Ibrahim toys with one of my pens. "I know everybody's supposed to bring their own food to the peace rally. But my mother and her friends, they just love cooking, so I figured I'd ask them to cook some food for all of us."

"Oh, yeah?" I salivate when I think of the yummy smells that always drift from the windows whenever I go to Ibrahim's neighborhood.

"It's a big deal for them. You know? Being involved and all. That's unusual. Anyway, just for you to know."

"That's cool, that's really cool," I say. The peace rally looks like a big deal for so many people, the enthusiastic ones or the opponents, that it gives me the creeps sometimes. Is it really a good idea and will it work?

Ibrahim slaps my arm. "Count on me," he says. "Saturday morning bright and early. We'll hang the banners."

"Thanks, I appreciate it."

"Relax," Ibrahim says. "I know how you feel. Waiting and all. My brother's now on a boat somewhere between Algeria and France."

"That's cool!"

"Except we don't know when he'll be home. My maman, she freaks out. You would think Mustafa's five! Come on, I tell her, he's a man!"

"I can't wait to see him," I say.

"Me neither," Ibrahim says. "Finally the big family all together." He nudges me with his shoulder. "I'll come to your place when it gets too suffocating."

"Anytime, dude," I say.

The café is quiet now that it's past seven o'clock. Garçon is mopping the floor when Richard bursts in.

"Got to go," Ibrahim says, and he slips away.

Richard spots me and walks over. "May I?" he asks, but he sits down before I say anything. "I was looking for you."

My heart flip-flops in my chest. "I thought we agreed on everything."

Richard leans back. "It's the fire department. They haven't yet said yes."

"What?"

Garçon sets a Coca-Cola in front of me. "That's what you need tonight."

I haven't had a coke here since the first time I set

foot in the café. Garçon turns to Richard. "I'll take care of the fire department," he says.

"You?" I say, clutching the neck of the bottle.

Garçon searches for my eyes. "You've come a long way, l'américain. Now it is my turn." He walks away, whistling as if we never had a conversation.

"What's up with him?" I ask Richard.

He shrugs and rubs his forehead. "Sometimes, *petit*," he says. "Even a cop has to leave some questions unanswered." He glances away.

I follow his eyes. Garçon stands behind the counter, rearranging his picture frames.

39 IN CONCERT AGAINST THE WAR

[*Sylvie, May 8, 1971:*]

Chocolat follows me from my room to the kitchen, and from the kitchen to the hallway, where I load several bags with the protest placards I finished last night. Each one of them displays the peace rally's slogan. Did I make too many? Not enough? If only I knew. Chocolat sniffs the bags and then pokes his head inside one. When the inspection is over, he drops to the floor and sighs.

Maman's sewing machine purrs, then stops. Her chair scrapes against the floor and she emerges from La Boutique.

"I can't force you to stay home," she says, taking off her thimble. "Half the town is going to this peace rally." She holds onto Chocolat's collar. "You stay here with us."

My dog blinks his liquid eyes. "Sorry, Chocolat," I say.

"Can I come?" Elle wears a T-shirt with a big peace sign that Stacey gave her.

Maman shakes her head. "You stay, too." She walks me to the door. "Be safe."

Scott and Detective Richard are kneeling over a map when I show up on the plaza at the stroke of one o'clock. They don't notice me when I drop my bags next to them. Early this morning, Scott and Ibrahim supervised the display of our banners. Now they hang between lampposts along rue Principale.

The message I wrote is featured on every single piece of advertising, and I feel weird reading it, now that the banners flap under the breeze. The posters Annie managed to display in town haven't been taken down. *It's a good sign*, I think, while I pace through the quiet streets of the early afternoon.

A few kids are chasing each other across the plaza. It's hard to know if within an hour a dozen or a hundred of people will show up. My heart catches in my throat when I think that nobody could come. Deep in thought, I've reached the bakery.

Annie bounds outside. "Ready?" she says, her cheeks flushed and her eyes shiny.

"Ready." I feel like I'm part of the French Résistance Mémé told me about, and excitement travels through my body.

Annie grabs my arm. "You know what?" she says, as the churches strike two o'clock. "It could be a day we'll remember for the rest of our lives."

By the time we return to the plaza, many people

have turned up. They gather in small groups, and their excited voices and laughter remind me of Bastille Day. People keep coming. Maman was right. Half the town must be here by now.

Brigitte hurries over. Two bulging bags bump against her sides. "I'm late," she says in a breathless voice. "They have just been delivered." She digs in her bags and pulls out a stack of T-shirts. "Can someone give me a hand, here?"

"Whoa!" Annie says. "They are really *chouette*." She slips one T-shirt on top of her own.

Once more, I'm awestruck to see my slogan printed on the T-shirts. I'm proud that I would pick the exact same words if I had to do it again today. I put one T-shirt on and hand them out to everyone around me.

"I want one!" Elle is weaving her way up to me.

"Papa and Maman changed their mind?" I say, looking around.

Elle shakes her head. "No, but they agreed I could come with Mémé for a little while. So can I get a T-shirt for Mémé too? And one for Stacey? And one for—"

"They'll get one when they show up," Brigitte says. "Don't worry, I've got plenty." She leans into me. "How many signs did you make?"

"Huh?" I have a hard time turning my mind away from thoughts of my parents.

"I've got two-hundred T-shirts," Brigitte says. "How many signs do you have?"

"Same."

Brigitte slaps her chest. "Thank you!" she says with a sigh of relief.

The crowd narrows around us. Hands reach for a T-shirt or a sign. A microphone crackles and spits out sound from the stage set in front of the statue of Jeanne d'Arc.

"Your attention, please!" Every head turns to the sound. Scott is perched on the stage, with dozens of people gathered at his feet.

"Thank you for coming," he says. "If you are here, it's because you oppose the Vietnam War …" Some people boo in response to his words. Scott taps the microphone for attention. "Today we are marching to honor the memory of four students who died a year ago on the campus of Kent University in Ohio, as they were peacefully protesting the war." He pauses as people get quiet. "Today is also the anniversary of the end of World War II. So we are marching united, French and Americans, because our people share the same hunger for peace. We are walking in concert against the war."

"End the war!" someone shouts, and soon many voices repeat as a chorus, "End the war!"

"The march," Scott goes on, "will start as soon as we've given away all the T-shirts and banners we've made. We'll march through downtown, then to the public park and the forest. A potluck dinner in the meadow will end the march."

Enthusiastic cheers welcome Scott. In the sea of

bodies, it's hard to recognize everyone, now that most of us wear the same T-shirts and wave the same banners. I only have a couple signs left when I spot the Colonel. I'm wondering if Scott talked him into coming, but I see Mémé holding his arm. A pair of oversized orange sunglasses swallows half of her face, and a matching hat frames her orange curls. She must have thought Woodstock instead of Château Moines when she picked her outfit.

"*Ma belle!*" Mémé plants a kiss on my cheek. "What a success! Almost like the Liberation after World War II! Isn't it, Colonel?"

"*Pfft,*" he says, straightening his jacket. "You exaggerate."

Mémé cups her hand around my ear and whispers, "I was able to convince him, but not your parents. Don't worry, *ma belle*, you're doing the right thing."

"*Merci*, Mémé," I say. She wipes off the lipstick mark she left on my cheek.

The Colonel taps the ground with his cane. "Shall we?" Mémé slips her arm under his, and she takes small steps to match his limping walk.

"Shall we?" Brigitte says, imitating his tone of voice.

"Wait!" Ibrahim is running toward us. "Sorry! I'm late!"

"The last T-shirt was for me," Brigitte says. "But you can have it."

Ibrahim slips it on and jogs toward Annie. "Thanks!" he shouts over his shoulder.

Brigitte and I elbow our way through the crowd. We bump into Monsieur Leroy and his wife. He flashes us the peace sign. *"Bravo, mes enfants!"*

Detective Richard is parked along the sidewalk, his eyes narrowing in the sun as he observes the mass of people passing by. A policeman stands at each corner of the plaza. The fire department has stationed several of their shiny trucks around town.

Château Moines's marching band and the majorettes agreed to perform when I asked them, and at the sound of the cymbals, everybody gets going. I find a quiet spot on the sidewalk, hoping despite all hope to recognize my parents in the crowd.

There is Mémé, holding the Colonel's arm. His collection of medals sparkles on his lapel. Stacey and Elle walk hand in hand with petit Paul and a bunch of kids from their school. They mimic the majorettes and throw their legs high in the air at the sound of the brass instruments. Monsieur Leroy and his wife hold each other's waists. Troubadour has brought his trumpet, and he plays with the band. I get a glimpse of Garçon, who has closed Chez Lili for the day. Scott's father and Mademoiselle Moulin follow right behind. Besides the peace sign, they carry a banner promoting a spring clothing donation for the Centre d'Assimilation pour Immigrants.

My parents' absence leaves a sour taste in my stomach, but people keep pouring along the street and I can't ignore them. Most are holding hands or linking arms, and all are chanting, "End the war!

Now! End the war! Now!"

Scott and Brigitte race to me. "Come on!" They grab both of my hands.

"Wait for us!" Ibrahim and Annie make a dash toward us.

"In Concert Against the War!" Scott says, linking his arm to mine.

We throw our arms up to the air. "In Concert Against the War!" we yell at the top of our lungs.

We aren't in Washington DC, New York City, San Francisco, or Los Angeles, but today Château Moines is just as big and important to me as they are. I glance at Brigitte, Ibrahim, Annie, and Scott. Despite our differences and where we are from, we've worked together toward a common goal.

In Concert Against the War. Hungry for World Peace. We Can Walk Anywhere Together.

So many words pour out of my mind that, despite my parents' absence, I feel happy, and I smile to myself.

40   A BIG MISTAKE

[*Scott:*]

Sylvie, Annie, and Brigitte have left me in charge of public relations, pretending they have to set the tables for the picnic. So here I am, greeting people I've never seen until now. They stop by to thank me, to tell me how important it is to get together to oppose violence. They even praise my French. Compliments pour all over me, and my face hurts as I smile like a movie star on the red carpet. *Thank you, merci!*

A few feet away, Ibrahim, surrounded by his little sisters and brothers and a group of kids from the projects, is in deep discussion with the librarian. I pretend not to be interested, but Ibrahim's voice catches my attention when he declares with great enthusiasm, "Without your involvement, Mademoiselle Moulin, most of us wouldn't have had any gifts. I hope you know how much we appreciate your work. From the bottom of my heart and all of my friends here today, thank you, Mademoiselle Moulin." He shakes her hand and the kids applaud.

I cringe in silence at each of Ibrahim's syrupy Mademoiselle Moulin this, Mademoiselle Moulin that. Did he transform himself into some kind of hypocrite? Also, when did he switch from a guy who spoke in two-word sentences to a wordy expert? I can't help stomping my Birkenstocks as I walk by the group. Big mistake! The librarian hears me, and I flinch at the shrieking sound of her voice.

"Scott!" I turn away, but her hand grabs my arm and I have to face her. "Scott!" she repeats. "What a day! Your father must be so proud!"

"Leave my father alone," I say.

Ibrahim fires a glance heavy with questions at me. The librarian stiffens, but manages a small wave when Sylvie joins us.

"Food's ready!" Sylvie announces with a big smile that freezes on her lips when she sees our faces. "What's wrong?"

"Nothing," I say.

"I was telling Scott how his father must be proud of him," the librarian says. "Being a generous man, he must only appreciate Scott's activism against the war."

Sylvie flashes me an encouraging smile. Of all people, she knows exactly what's going on with that woman, and I appreciate her silent support. I back up, but the librarian steps forward.

"We've established stronger foundations since

your father's involvement," she says. "He's so committed." I swear if she says one more word I'll barf.

Ibrahim jumps in. "Come on, Scott. With your father's help, the Centre d'Assimilation has done more in one winter than in a year."

They both look at me like I'm some sort of brat, but I also read some pity in their eyes, and I can't stand it.

"I'm tired of you telling me that my father is a saint," I say.

"It's all right," the librarian says in a patient voice.

"Come on," Ibrahim says in a soothing tone.

So, that's it, now they believe I lost it and pity me. Sylvie is watching me like she is discovering something about me she doesn't like.

"Can you speak plain French and tell me what's on your mind?" I say.

The sound of my voice jolts people. Fortunately they think it is part of a gig or something, and they return to their conversations.

Ibrahim shifts his eyes from me to the librarian, like he is trying to find the right approach to calm me down.

"You know," he says. "She really appreciates your father."

"How surprising," I say.

"She can't stop thanking Hollywood Follies."

I grab his arm. "Seriously, what has exactly my father done that is so remarkable?"

Ibrahim sighs, as if I were the dumbest person he ever met. "The clothes," he says with another exaggerated sigh. "For the holiday season."

Horrified by what he just said, I let go off his arm. I don't need to think twice to realize how wrong I've been. The librarian, my father, their mysterious conversations, and the wrapped Christmas packages, everything makes sense, and I feel awful.

"You didn't know?" Ibrahim says. "Your father donated jeans, T-shirts, jewelry, and all kinds of cool stuff so each of us in the projects had a gift for the holidays."

My silence says more than any words. Sylvie looks at me with a mixture of pity and disappointment, and I wonder if she will ever forgive me for having tarnished the image of her beloved librarian.

41 WHERE IS ELLE?

[Sylvie:]

Brigitte hands me a bowl of potato chips. I take one chip, but I'm not hungry. How could Scott be so sure of himself when he accused Mademoiselle Moulin of pursuing his father? How could he ignore the fact that his father was only helping her? I feel angry with him for convincing me that Mademoiselle Moulin wasn't who she seemed to be. In the end, she is the great person I knew all along she was, but I believed Scott. How could I not trust my instincts and tell him he was wrong?

"*Ça va?*" Brigitte says, looking down at my hands.

I've crushed the potato chip to dust. I walk away before Brigitte asks me another question. All around me people talk, laugh, and eat. We couldn't have picked a better day or a better spot, but Scott's ridiculous suspicions make me sick. I pace the meadow and reach the food area.

Ibrahim has signed up for the food booth, and he's already cooked a batch of North African sausages called *merguez*. Annie is loading plates with the thin spicy sausages, which a bunch of girls offer to the people.

"Can you take over for me for a second?" Ibrahim says. His face glistens with sweat. "I'm so hot I can't tell what is cooking, them or me." He hands me a pair of tongs and rushes to get some water.

"Is it good?" Scott is eyeing the merguez.

"Be my guest," I say, handing him a fork without looking at him.

He takes a bite. "Tasty." Then, he grimaces. "Hot! What's inside?"

Annie giggles, and I shrug. Garçon steps over and borrows my tongs.

"*Merguez* are made of beef and lamb," he explains, flipping them on the grill.

"And tons of spices," Scott says, fanning his mouth.

Garçon laughs. "Otherwise they would be called hotdogs, l'américain."

"French cuisine can be so overrated," Scott says, pouring a large glass of water.

"Don't drink!" Garçon pulls the glass out of Scott's reach. "Eat this." He hands him a chunk of bread. "For your information, this is Mediterranean cuisine. Merguez came here via North Africa."

Scott stuffs his mouth with the bread. "Why didn't anybody tell me?" He shoots me accusing glares.

"Some discoveries hurt," I say.

Scott grabs a handful of potato chips. "Are we even now?"

"That was harsh, how you talked to Mademoiselle Moulin," I say. "I know you've got excuses and it was easy to assume something was going on. Still."

Scott bows in front of me. "Does your highness grant me pardon?"

I look away in a disdainful way, but I can't help a smile.

"Sorry for my mistake," he says, his eyes still tearing up from the spices. "And thanks for your help. I wouldn't have done the rally if you hadn't told me about May '68."

"May '68?" Annie hands us a plate of merguez. "What did Sylvie tell you?"

"You know," Scott says. "The strikes, the barricades, and all."

I swat my hand at a fly, while Annie slaps her thigh and bursts out in laughter.

"In May '68, we biked all day long because we had no school. The weather was great and we played in the forest." A fit of hiccups stops her.

Scott looks at me and our eyes meet. "You didn't do anything, go anywhere, or see anything?" His voice carries the hope that Annie is the liar, not me.

"Oh, I forgot," Annie goes on. "We also watched TV." She has regained control of herself. "Nothing happened here in May '68. We only had a vacation before summer vacation. That was *chouette*; right,

Sylvie?"

I nod, unable to add anything, unable to meet Scott's stare. When I realize that I am a liar and would never have admitted it to Scott if Annie hadn't opened her big mouth, I take off, leaving Scott, Annie, and a needed explanation behind me.

The sun is setting and the air smells of barbeque and grass. Kids run all over the meadow. I hear Mémé laugh. Groups of adults are sitting under the trees. Ibrahim's mother and her friends are cooking some lamb and chicken. Teams of girls and boys from school carry heaping plates to everyone. It smells of a happy day, and I ruined it.

I look for Elle, but only spot Stacey and petit Paul. Janis Joplin's raspy voice floods the meadow. A roll of thunder covers the song. People peer at the sky and someone says, "Oh, no, I hope we won't get a storm."

Everybody is glancing up, but the sky remains silent. Someone puts on another record and cranks up the volume. Simon and Garfunkel's guitars resonate in the meadow.

This is Scott's favorite music, and I wish I could rewind the film of the afternoon and be dancing with him now. Many people have jumped to their feet at the sound of the music. Mémé and the Colonel are holding each other's waists. Garçon has invited Mademoiselle Moulin to dance. Annie and Ibrahim walk by, hand in hand. I peel my eyes for my sister, but don't see her.

Another roll of thunder explodes in the sky, just as I hear Stacey's panicked screaming.

"Elle! Elle! Where is Elle?"

42   A STRANGER IN TOWN

[*Scott:*]

The Colonel points to the volunteers with his cane. "Team One: twenty people in town. Team Two: twenty people through the park. The little one can't be far. Go!"

Annie's foster dad leads Team One to town. Dad and Troubadour join Team Two. Garçon tags along. Richard gathers the kids around him.

"You," he says, pointing at Annie and Ibrahim, "take the kids and search the meadow!"

Sylvie has turned into a statue. Even her skin is the color of clay. Although I'm disappointed in her, I can only imagine how I would feel if Stacey had disappeared.

"She can't be far," I say, repeating the Colonel's words.

"I should've watched for her," Sylvie says.

Her grandmother staggers toward us, leaning on the Colonel. "Oh, Sylvie," she says. "I don't understand. She was there one second and gone the next. Where could she be?" She runs a trembling hand through her hair, while the Colonel holds the other. "I must get your parents."

"I'll do it, Mémé," Sylvie says.

"I'll come with you," I say.

We take off, leaving the Colonel and Richard in charge.

Sylvie presses the doorbell until Madame Pottier, Chocolat on her heels, unlocks the door. A long piece of white fabric is draped over her shoulder and a pair of scissors sticks from her pocket.

"What's wrong?" she says, eyeing me with suspicion.

"We can't find Elle," Sylvie says.

"What!" Madame Pottier says. The fabric slips to the ground. The dog looks up and barks plaintively. "Denis!" Madame Pottier calls in a matching wailing voice.

"I'm sorry," Sylvie says.

"It's not your fault if your sister wandered away," I say.

Madame Pottier's eyes widen with terror and accusation. "She didn't wander away. Someone took her."

"Maman," Sylvie says. "I didn't say that."

Madame Pottier holds so tightly onto the doorjamb that her knuckles are white. "I had my reasons to oppose this peace thing. I shouldn't have listened to Mémé."

Monsieur Pottier pokes his disheveled head into the room. "What's going on?" His eyes dart from Sylvie to his wife and then rest on me. "What's wrong, son?" he asks me, realizing I'm the calmest of all.

"It's Elle, monsieur, she was at the rally, but now we can't find her."

He has slipped his jacket on before I finish my sentence. The four of us rush out behind Chocolat, who leads us to the park. Voices calling for Elle echo around us, while we make our way to the meadow.

"I'll search for her," Monsieur Pottier tells his wife. "Don't worry, she can't be far." His voice is firm, but his eyes are full of worry. "I'll be right back."

"Let's ask Stacey if she knows something," Sylvie tells me. Chocolat sticks to her and the three of us take off, Madame Pottier following behind.

"When was the last time you saw Elle?" Sylvie asks my sister.

"I don't know," Stacey says, holding tight onto the hand of petit Paul.

"Where did Elle go?" Sylvie insists.

Stacey sticks her thumb in her mouth. Tears pearl up in her eyes. Petit Paul pulls his handkerchief from his pocket. "Here you go, Stacey."

"Where did she go?" Madame Pottier says, leaning in towards Stacey's face.

"Leave her alone!" I shout. Petit Paul jumps, but my sister doesn't even look at me. It breaks my heart to see her sucking her thumb. It took her four months to quit that after Mom passed away.

"What's the matter with you?" Sylvie tells me. "My sister has disappeared and we can't ask her best friend when she saw her last?"

"She must know something," Madame Pottier says. "They're always together."

"She says she doesn't know," I say, wrapping an arm around my sister's shoulders. "She can't even think." I pull Stacey toward me.

Sylvie and her mother back up. Dark clouds tumble over us, and rolls of thunder drown the children's voices calling for Elle.

A booming voice jolts us. "I found him!" Monsieur Pottier pushes a stumbling young man ahead of him. The man drags a beat-up suitcase and a couple of plastic bags.

"Who is he?" Madame Pottier examines the stranger's face.

"Found him wandering in town, unable to say anything coherent!" A vein pulses in Monsieur Pottier's neck.

The Colonel limps towards us. "What is it, Pottier?" he asks, breathless.

"I found him! Alone, with his suitcase." Monsieur Pottier is all worked up. His hand grips the young man's collar. "He's none of us, right?"

"Who are you? Where do you come from?" The Colonel waves a flashlight across the young man's face.

He shades his eyes with his hand. "Mustafa," he mumbles. "From Marseilles."

The name sounds familiar, and in a flash I remember Ibrahim telling me about his brother being somewhere between Algeria and France. I look for my friend, but people crowd around Monsieur Pottier, Mustafa, and the Colonel, and I can't see Ibrahim.

"He's Ibrahim's brother," I shout.

"So what?" Monsieur Pottier tightens his grip on the man's arm.

"Where is my daughter?" Madame Pottier screams. "What have you done to her?"

"Don't know what you are talking about," Mustafa says. He shakes his head as if its weight was unbearable. "Ask my family."

"What family?" The vein in Monsieur Pottier's neck throbs like a naked heart.

"Who are you?" Madame Pottier's voice breaks down.

"He told you!" I shout again. "He's Ibrahim's brother." I turn around, hoping to spot my friend, but he's nowhere to be seen.

"What's going on here?" In two large strides, Richard has reached us. He's followed by a group of men and women.

"Found this guy in town," Monsieur Pottier says. "Can't talk properly. Can't answer my questions. I tell you, prime suspect."

"Keep your hands off this man," Richard says.

"And let him answer my questions."

Monsieur Pottier hesitates, but he lets go of the man's shirt. Everyone backs up and Richard steps forward. "What's your name, fellow?"

"Mustafa," the young man says. "Mustafa Maarouf."

I catch some movement in the crowd and hear comments, now that everyone finally understands he's part of the Maarouf family.

"*Et voilà!*" Richard tips his hat. "Can I see your papers?"

The young man shivers, as thunder booms through town. He rummages in his pants pockets and pats his jacket. "Maybe in my suitcase?" he says.

I'm getting nervous as I follow his search. "He said he's a Maarouf," I say, but nobody pays attention until a man approaches.

"Mustafa is my son," he says. In his hands he's holding a wallet. "He has papers."

Ibrahim's mother steps forward. "Our son has papers," she says, bringing her hand to her husband's arm. "We do, too. Show them our papers," she urges her husband.

"Then," a familiar voice shouts from the crowd. "Why can't he prove it?"

"He's tired," Ibrahim's mother says. "The bus comes from Marseilles. It's a long journey after the boat from Algeria." She glances with fear around her. "He has papers," she says one more time.

"He's my brother!" Ibrahim splits the crowd and

leaps to his brother. "He's my brother!" he shouts, facing the crowd. A big proud grin illuminates his face.

"Doesn't mean he shouldn't have papers!" the same man shouts. I recognize Garçon's voice, and I don't like what's happening now.

Ibrahim and his brother hug and talk at the same time.

"Speak in French!" Garçon hollers. "We don't know what they are talking about when they speak in their native tongue."

"As far as I know he's a stranger," Monsieur Pottier says. "Without an I.D."

The crowd buzzes in agreement. I catch Richard's worried look and see how his hand slides underneath his trenchcoat. Everything inside me turns upside down.

He can only be looking for his gun.

43 PEACE STARTS AT HOME

[*Sylvie:*]

Tell you what," Detective Richard says in a casual tone, his hand hooked around his belt, while Mustafa fumbles through his suitcase. "I'm taking you downtown. You'll empty your suitcase, you'll find your papers, and you'll go home to your family."

"Leave him alone," Ibrahim says in a quivering voice. "I've searched the meadow. Elle isn't there. My brother has nothing to do with her disappearance." He looks around and spots Annie. "Tell them!" he shouts.

"That's right," Annie says. Her cheeks are flushed and she's out of breath. "We haven't found Elle, and this guy wasn't even there when she left the meadow."

"Trust me, it will be easier if Mustafa comes with me." Detective Richard closes the suitcase with his foot.

"You can't do that!" Ibrahim steps between the detective and his brother. Annie follows him and tries to pull him away. He jerks his arm free.

"Don't worry," Mustafa says, squeezing Ibrahim's shoulder. "Just a quick verification."

A satisfied humming rises from the mass of people.

"This is wrong!" Ibrahim pumps his fist to the sky. "My brother didn't do anything. He was on a bus when Elle disappeared!"

"Trust me," Detective Richard repeats. "It's safer for your brother to come with me. These people are too agitated for their own good."

"I'll prove all of you wrong!" Ibrahim pushes Annie away, forces his way through the people, and takes off.

Annie shoots me a dark look, as if I were responsible for what was happening. Does she think that because I bragged about my talents as an activist I am a liar? Panic and guilt mix in my head. I'm sure that Mustafa has nothing to do with Elle's disappearance. I'm also sure that nothing would have happened if I hadn't agreed to help with this rally. People crowd around Detective Richard, pressing and shoving as if they were starving and trying to get a loaf of bread. Only now they are after a man. They shout and the circle narrows around them. Detective Richard tries to move away, only to meet my father's strong grip.

"Tell us where the little girl is," a woman yells. I

crane my neck and recognize the florist.

"What did you do to her?" Garçon spits in Mustafa's direction.

It's scary to see the familiar faces of friendly business people all worked up. A knot rises to my throat when bodies push against me. Detective Richard is using his arm as a shield to protect Mustafa from the crowd. I elbow my way out of the circle just in time to escape the tidal wave that moves people forward against their individual will. They clash against each other and the circle tightens around Mustafa. I see fists raised in the air and hear screams that smell and taste of hate and fear. The wave is pulsing as loud as my heart in my ears.

Detective Richard brandishes his pistol in the air and the crowd backs up at once. The same scared and angry sounds come out of their mouths.

"Stop it!" I yell and my own voice surprises me. "Stop it!"

Nobody hears me in the tumult of the shouts and the strength of the crowd.

I spot the microphone Scott used earlier today and yank at it. "Stop it!" I shout, and people search for the direction of the voice. Annie makes her way closer to me.

I tap the mike. "Please!" I start. "We can't walk for world peace and be violent."

"This man is violent!" Garçon yells. His words are followed by grunts of agreement.

Mustafa has dropped to the ground, holding his

head between his hands. His body is shrinking, now as small and beat-up as his suitcase, spilling its contents onto the ground. Detective Richard has already put his weapon away.

"Mustafa has done nothing," I say. Now that I have everyone's attention, I don't need to shout anymore. "He told us his name and where he is from. He is frightened and nervous and can't find his papers. Is it a reason to accuse him? My sister has disappeared, and I'm scared. But I refuse to blame someone just because he is new and comes from Algeria."

A rumor rolls through the mass of people at the name of Algeria, and I tighten my hand around the microphone to stay calm. "Remember why we are here today. We've walked hand in hand against a bloody war that has already taken too many lives. Although it is happening kilometers away from us, we wanted to protest against it. We can't allow ourselves to become violent and prejudiced."

"She's right!" Annie shouts, and I look for her. I'm so glad she stands up for me.

"That's just words!" Garçon's strong voice booms. "This man shows up when a little one disappears. I don't buy coincidence. He must have done something. Look at him! He's guilty as hell!"

The crowd hums as the tone of his voice rises. I can't let his hateful words wash over me and drown my own words. I brandish my mike.

"We have no reason to believe that Mustafa did

anything wrong. What's happening now is wrong! It's based on nothing." And Maman's words come to my lips. "Peace starts at home," I say, and the words sound right and perfect.

Thunder rolls through town. Detective Richard is staring at me; his hand is resting on Mustafa's neck, but his fingers aren't pulling onto the collar of his shirt. With a gentle push, he helps Mustafa to his feet. Papa extends his arm so close to Mustafa's face he could touch him. Or punch him. A low murmur rises from the people, but when I believe they will encourage my father to hit Mustafa, they suddenly part to let Detective Richard lead Mustafa away. Their silence is as threatening as their screams were seconds ago. Thunder growls. A fat drop of water hits my forehead.

Both churches ring nine o'clock when my mother shouts, "Where were you when my little girl disappeared?" She is launching herself toward Scott's father. "If it's not the Arab man, it can only be you!"

Papa grabs her arm. "Simone!" But his voice can't cover her screams.

Maman claws her hand onto Mademoiselle Moulin's sleeve. "And you? Where were you?"

Mademoiselle Moulin reaches for my mother. "We were looking for Elle."

"Don't talk about Elle," Maman says. "Since these people came, nothing is the same. Even you have changed." Her shoulders are trembling, and she crumples into Papa's arms.

I'm so ashamed of my mother that I keep my eyes down. Yet her pain touches me and words pour out of my heart as the sky bursts open above our heads.

Raindrops are the sky's teardrops.

Tears are the rain of the heart.

Madame Duval rushes over with an umbrella, which she uses to protect Annie from the rain. She gently pats my arm. "Your mother is upset," she says. "It's understandable. I'm sure we'll find Elle." She pulls Annie to her and, for once, I notice that Annie snuggles closer as they walk away.

Everyone runs for his life as the rain beats down on us, but I don't move until a zigzag of lightning slashes the sky. The sound of whistles and calls for Elle pierce the silence of the night. An owl ululates and a dog barks in the distance. I look for Chocolat, but can't see him. I grab a flashlight that was left on a table. Nobody sees me sprinting into the forest. Before I know it, the night has swallowed me.

The entrance to the forest is a gigantic mouth opened onto the dark. It closes on me as soon as I step ahead. Rain bombards my skin like pellets. The wind covers my voice as I call for Elle. I trip on tree roots and twice I fall to my knees.

The flashlight flickers several times before fading. The batteries are getting weaker by the second, and they die just when I reach la cabane.

I search for the knob and turn it. Locked.

I lean against the window. A flash of lightning illuminates the clearing. I peek inside. Empty.

Even if Elle came here, she has gone. I retrace my steps to the path. The river has already swollen, and the sound of the rushing water fills my ears. The night is thicker beneath the trees, and I can't wait to be back to the meadow. Without the flashlight, I stagger and I have to feel for the trees to stay on the path. A branch smacks my face, leaving a stinging welt on my cheek. Twigs snap around me, and I jump at the sound.

"Elle!" I call. "Elle! Where are you? Elle!"

Leaves rustle and branches crack as if someone had followed me and was now spying on me. A flashlight cuts through the night. I press my hand against my chest. My heart is leaping out of me. A dark shape bounds out of the bushes.

"Chocolat!" An immediate feeling of safety washes over me.

My dog's breath is short and raspy and his drenched coat smells of mud. "What happened? Where have you been?"

Another branch snaps, and I freeze. "Elle! Is that you?"

Footsteps answer my call.

Chocolat barks and nudges me until I follow him. Wind slaps my face, and I hurry behind my dog. He turns around, waits for me, and resumes his speed until I find myself face to face with Ibrahim. He's carrying my sister in his arms.

"Elle!" I slam my hand to my mouth.

One of her arms is draped around Ibrahim's neck.

The other one falls limply against his side. Mud is spread on my sister's face and bare legs.

I put my hand to her chest and feel for a heartbeat. "Where did you find her?"

Ibrahim's face is as dirty as Elle. "The dog did," he says. His breathing is short. He looks exhausted. "In a ravine. We've got to get help."

The storm is moving away. The clouds are making way for the stars. One by one they shine in the sky. Drops of rain trickle from the branches and leaves. I sweep Ibrahim's flashlight in front of me, making sure we aren't straying away from the path. The owl I heard earlier is flying above us. Once in a while I glance above my shoulder, checking on Ibrahim and Elle. I speed up when I spot the lights of town, wavering between the trees.

"I'm going too fast?" I ask Ibrahim.

In two strides, he has matched his pace to mine. "Soccer practice makes it easy."

The path widens. Above my head, the owl flaps his wings and flies away when we reach the meadow.

"Help! Help!" I yell.

Annie is the first one to jump to her feet. "Ibrahim! Ibrahim found Elle!"

44 SAFE AND SOUND

[*Scott:*]

Garçon has opened Chez Lili, and everyone has gathered inside. I've looked everywhere for Sylvie. What she did is really amazing. I want to tell her that although she knew nothing about May '68, she has managed to stop a riot, and it's much more important. But I only see her mother, Mémé, and the Colonel, huddling together.

Stacey is sucking her thumb on Dad's lap. The rest of the world doesn't exist anymore, and her behavior reminds me so much of what happened after Mom died that I'm terrified. Mademoiselle Moulin ruffles her hair, and my sister cuddles closer to Dad.

"Help! Help!" We all turn at once at the sound of Ibrahim's voice.

Annie is the first one to jump to her feet. "Ibrahim! Ibrahim found Elle!"

Elle's long hair is spilling down Ibrahim's left arm.

His right arm is slung underneath her limp legs. Their clothes and faces are caked with mud. I catch a glimpse of Sylvie and Chocolat standing right behind them. Grimy water drips from Chocolat's coat. A branch has slashed Sylvie's forehead and dirt stains her jeans. In a second, Annie and everyone are surrounding them.

"*Mon cœur!*" Sylvie's mother yanks Elle from Ibrahim.

A paramedic splits the crowd, a stethoscope dangling around his neck. "Let me examine your daughter first." Madame Pottier holds tight on Elle. "Madame, please."

Monsieur Pottier rushes over and wraps an arm around his wife's shoulders. "It's all right," he says. "It's all right."

Elle is a rag doll in the paramedic's muscular arms. Garçon has cleared a table, on which the paramedic lays Elle down. The whole room is holding its breath while he checks her heartbeat. Elle flutters her eyelids. Her eyes wander around and rest on Sylvie. A smile turns her lips up when she recognizes her sister.

Madame and Monsieur Pottier lean above Elle. "You're alive, *merci, mon Dieu!*"

I wrap my arm around Stacey's shoulders. "Elle's okay," I say.

She quivers under my touch. "She's not dead?"

"No, she's just tired. And very dirty." I give a gentle squeeze to her shoulder. "Don't worry."

Stacey looks up at me. Her eyes hesitate before

resting on my face. "I don't remember anything after Elle left."

"It's okay." I stroke her hair, which feels knotty between my fingers. "You need a shampoo," I say, and Stacey smiles her Mom's grin.

Garçon has invited all of us for a warm drink. He sees me and freezes, his tray loaded with cups of steaming coffee and hot chocolate. Annie walks over.

"For Ibrahim," Garçon says, handing her a cup of cocoa, before moving to the crowded tables.

I follow Annie to the back of the café, where we find Ibrahim, leaning against the Foosball table. Mud lines his face, and his hair is plastered against his skull. His jeans are wet to the knees.

"That's for you," Annie says, giving him the cup of cocoa.

"Hey," I say. "You found Elle."

A shadow passes over his dark eyes. "My brother has done nothing."

"I know."

"Everyone knows it," Annie says. Ibrahim gives a small laugh.

"The dog," he says. "He found Elle."

"Right," Annie says. "Chocolat is a sweet dog. I'm not so sure he would make the rescue team."

Ibrahim ignores her comment and sniffs the air. "Dude, you need a bath," he tells me.

My T-shirt smells like a wet towel, my jeans are as stiff as a cardboard box, and I dream of a hot shower. I slap him on the back and he flops onto a chair.

"You too, dude."

I slide in next to him. "You're a hero, dude."

"The dog," he says, stretching his legs onto another chair.

Annie sits down, leaning her back against Ibrahim's legs. People in the café are talking and laughing, but we are quiet and it feels perfect. Someone has brought up an old French song on the jukebox. Chez Lili smells of wet wool and it's as cozy as home. Now that Elle is safe, I drift away.

I think Ibrahim is asleep when he shifts on his chair and yawns. "Elle," he says. "She said something. Sounded like *la cabane*. Any idea what she's talking about?"

Annie sits up straight.

"I suppose I owe you two an explanation. See, in the fall—"

"You don't owe me anything," Ibrahim says, with a yawn.

"Right," Annie says, and she leans back.

Sylvie pokes her head in at the doorway. The café pulses with music, voices, laughter, and with Annie and Ibrahim's snores. Sylvie drags a chair next to mine and throws a blanket around our shoulders.

And the two of us snuggle in the warmth of our silent conversation.

45 AN INVITATION FOR THE TOWN

[*Sylvie, May 9, 1971:*]

Elle spoons a heaping ladle of mashed potatoes onto her plate. "I told you everything," she says, her mouth full.

Papa pours some red wine into Maman's glass and fills my sister's glass and mine with water. "The most important thing is to have you home," he says. "Forget about what happened."

"Right," Maman says. She takes a sip of her wine and dabs the corners of her mouth with her napkin. "The best way to recoup is to rest."

"Again?" Elle says with a sigh. "I don't want to rest. I want to see Stacey. I have a lot to tell her. She has no idea what I—" She stops midsentence and shoots me a side look.

"You've got plenty of time to see Stacey," Papa says. "You have to put everything behind you first."

"But I don't want to forget anything."

"Weren't you scared?" Papa's eyes are red from

the lack of sleep and the worry.

"A little." Elle shrugs. "The storm was really scary and the wolf too."

"How could you think Chocolat was a wolf?" I ask, and Chocolat of course barks to show his agreement. "He saved you."

"Ibrahim saved me," Elle says with a beaming look on her face.

"I've been thinking," Maman says. "This boy acted like a true hero."

"No," Elle says. "He acts like a true professional soccer player." I can't help but laugh. "That's true," Elle insists. "Stop making fun of me."

"Someone who saves someone else's life is a hero," Papa says.

"Since we all agree he's a hero," Maman says, "I want to invite him and his family for dinner."

Silence follows her words. If I had my notebook, I would write down the song titles that flood my mind.

Unexpected Hero. Unexpected Dinner Guests. Guess Who's Coming to Dinner Tonight?

Elle jumps from her chair and paces the kitchen. "Can Stacey come too? And petit Paul? Also—"

"Good idea," Maman says. "We should invite every person who looked for you."

Now we are all up, talking at the same time. I get some paper. Papa finds a pen. Maman flips the calendar open. Elle saunters across the kitchen. I feel like the day Scott and I set the date for the peace rally. Only now, it's in my home, with my family, who never does anything spontaneous and never has anyone visit our home, except Mémé and Maman's brides-to-be. Excitement and hope creep inside me, first slowly and timidly, then faster and bolder, and in the end they burst out of me, joyful and impatient.

Papa sets his pen down when our list is complete. "I didn't know we knew so many people," he says.

Maman peeks at the list. "I know everyone. I just stopped seeing them."

I catch some sadness in her voice, and I use my most cheerful voice to say, "Let me call everyone!"

The following days look like nothing I've known so far. Papa mows the lawn as short as the Colonel's buzz cut. The garage is so clean we could eat off the ground. Maman is buried in her cookbooks. Even Mémé gets involved in the RSVP business, since Maman preferred the old-fashioned mailed invitations rather than my phone calls.

Two days before the big day, everybody has RSVP'd but the Maaroufs.

"They have a big family," Mémé tells Maman. "They must be overwhelmed."

"Still." Maman sounds disappointed.

But Ibrahim shows up before dinner that very same day. "My family wants to help," he says, when Maman opens the front door.

"No way," Maman says.

Ibrahim sighs. "You don't understand."

"You are our guests."

Ibrahim skips from one foot to another. "We have

to. It's our tradition."

"Bread, then," Maman says. "Bring bread."

Ibrahim looks down and then up. He catches my eyes, and I know bread won't work. "My parents and my brother want to do the *méchoui*," he says.

"The what?"

"The *méchoui*."

"Oh, *non, non, non, non, non,*" Maman says, shaking her head like a weather vane.

"What's a *méchoui*?" Elle asks.

"A roasted lamb," Ibrahim says. "You'll love it."

"Please, Maman!" Elle jumps up and down.

"Elle should choose," I say, and Ibrahim mouths *merci*.

"I'm not sure," Maman says.

"Please, Maman!" Elle repeats until Maman says oui.

On Saturday morning, we wake up early so we can clean up again and prepare the desserts. Cleaning is done by noon, so the rest of the afternoon smells of cooked apples, caramel, and chocolate. By the end of the day, we've prepared enough chocolate mousse, crème caramel, and compotes to feed hundreds, and we've baked enough pies and cakes to open our own bakery. Chocolat wanders across the kitchen like a drunk high on sugar.

Maman shoos us to bed early. "Tomorrow will be a long day," she says, switching the lights off.

"You are sleeping?" Elle whispers as soon as the door is closed. I remain silent. "Sylvie?"

278

I turn my bedside table lamp on. "Yes, I'm asleep, thanks for asking."

Elle fluffs her pillow and sits in her bed. "You don't want to write?"

I shoot her a dark look. "Did you read my notebook, too?"

"I swear I didn't," she says, raising her hand.

"I'm supposed to believe someone who snoops through people's lives?"

"You never do anything with me," Elle says with a sniff. "One day I was angry at you, so I followed you and Scott." She pushes her blanket away and gets to my side of the room. "Are you angry at me?" She sits on my bed and in the light of my lamp, her face appears small and anxious.

Funny, but I've never been angry with Elle. Annoyed, yes, often; and worried oh, yes, very worried; but never mad at her.

"I never thought you would have the guts to go to the forest alone," I say.

"I even went inside la cabane once."

That clears Annie for good, I realize, and my heart flutters with relief.

"The day of the peace rally," Elle says. "I told Stacey I had something to show her. But she wanted to dance with petit Paul, so I left alone. I thought I'd remember the way to la cabane, but I got lost and then it rained." She pauses and sighs. "And then the wolf came and—"

"Can you sleep, now that you've told me

everything?"

Elle climbs into her bed. "I'm glad you aren't mad."

"Can you be quiet?"

"I will. I swear." And she is, while I open my trunk, and pick up my pen and my notebook. "Are you writing?" she asks.

"No, I'm doing my math homework."

"Liar!" she says with a small giggle.

I write for a few minutes. "You want to hear what I wrote?" I ask. A small snore answers me, and I tuck my notebook away.

Too bad Elle is asleep, I think, as I close my eyes on a promising song.

46 MÉCHOUI

[*Scott, May 22, 1971:*]

Stacey checks out my outfit and nods her approval. "And don't forget your guitar!"

"What about you?" I point at her pair of ragged denim shorts and stained white T-shirt.

She rolls her eyes. "Don't worry about me. Hurry up."

"You aren't even close to being ready," I say, but she saunters away, humming a French love song she and Elle adore for some reason.

Dad pokes his head in. "Time to go, son."

When I show up in the living room, carrying my guitar and my music, Stacey is all dressed up and tapping her foot on the floor. "Hurry up! We'll be late."

She's wearing a lot of yellow, and she makes me think of a sun. I doubt she'll take that as a compliment so I say, "Nice blouse."

"It's a tunic," she says with a pout.

"Whatever, it's nice."

"Girls!" Dad says with a smile and a shrug in my direction.

Stacey and I wear our roller skates, so Dad has to run to keep up with us. By the time we reach Sylvie's home, her front yard buzzes with people. I take my skates off and right away spot many people I know. Brigitte is here, as well as Annie and her foster parents. Sylvie is helping her mom, and Ibrahim stands next to a deep pit. He tips his Dodgers cap when he sees me.

"My brother Mustafa," he says, introducing me to an older version of himself. He looks nothing like the guy who was scared and panicked two weeks ago when Elle disappeared.

Mustafa shakes my hand. "*Bonjour*," he says with a warm smile. "You must be Scott."

"He knows everything about you," Ibrahim says, elbowing me.

"Only good stuff," Mustafa adds when he sees my face. "Now, if you don't mind, I have to take care of this animal."

A whole lamb is roasting above the fire burning in the pit. On the other side of the yard, Ibrahim's father is turning the spit while his mother is basting another lamb with juices. Some of his little sisters and brothers hold utensils for them.

"Hope we'll have enough food for everyone," Ibrahim says, with a worried glance toward the crowd gathering in the yard.

"Looks like plenty to me." Platters of cheese, bowls filled with different salads, and baskets of bread are piled on several tables.

"You don't know the French," Ibrahim says, taking his turn at the spit.

"Do you need help?"

"So far, so good." Ibrahim shoos me away. "Go and have fun."

The smells of roasted meat and fries, of cheese and ripe fruit, of pies and cakes make my stomach gurgle. I look for Sylvie and I see her standing behind a table that has been set up for the drinks. Garçon has brought pitchers from the café, and he and Sylvie serve water, lemonade, and fruit punch to a bunch of kids crowding around them.

Troubadour slaps my back, eyeing my guitar. "How is it going, Santana?"

"It's going."

"Maybe some lessons this summer?"

"Maybe," I say.

Business has picked up over the last weeks. Dad says that since the peace rally he now has a few regular customers and that more people stop by. I see him walking toward me with Mademoiselle Moulin, Stacey, and Elle.

"Thank you for searching for me," Elle says, holding her small hand out.

I take it and shake it. "You know, it's Ibrahim who deserves your thank-you."

"He's my hero!" She gallops away, followed by my sister.

Dad hands me a plate loaded with a juicy slice of lamb, some couscous, some beans, and a piece of crusty bread. "Eat," he says.

Mademoiselle Moulin has brought a blanket and the three of us sit on together. The food is so good that we don't talk for a few minutes, and it's all right with me. I'm still embarrassed at thinking the two of them were more than friends, and I haven't had the guts to talk with my father about it, much less to apologize.

"Huh," I say to him, looking down at my plate. "That's cool what you did for Christmas, you know, the clothes, the gifts. I had no idea."

"I'll go get some drinks," Mademoiselle Moulin says.

Dad sets his plate down. "Let me help."

"*Non, non,*" she says, putting her hand on Dad's shoulder to keep him seated. "Enjoy your meal with your son."

When she's gone, Dad clears his throat. "I should have told you. So much was going on already that I didn't want to overwhelm you with more things." He searches for my eyes. "I needed to do things on my own, but I'm sorry for keeping my activities from you."

It's noisy and warm around us, and I don't feel like talking. I'm not sure Dad expects a comment from me anyway. We polish off the food on our plates without another word. I take my sandals off and lie down on the blanket, facing the big blue sky and its fat, lazy clouds.

"Why don't you go see your friends?" Dad asks.

I sit up and I spot all of them around the fire. I doubt they noticed my absence, but I know Dad means well. It's not worth starting a discussion about it, so I stand up, slip my sandals on, and drag my sorry self to the fire pit.

"Hey, Scott!" I turn back at the sound of Dad's voice. He flashes a peace sign. "You brought peace here!"

I shrug, but flash the peace sign too.

"Listen, everybody!" A voice bellows across the yard.

It takes a couple of minutes for people to spot Sylvie's father up on a chair. He clinks his fork against his glass to call for attention.

"Listen, everybody!" He waits for total silence. "Two weeks ago, my little girl Elle got lost. It was the scariest day of my life." He clears his throat. "But thanks to a courageous boy, she was found safe and sound." He looks around, searching for a face in the crowd.

"Please, no!" Ibrahim hides behind me.

"Too late, dude," I say.

"Ibrahim Maarouf, come on over!" Monsieur Pottier has spotted Ibrahim. "You saved my little girl and you deserve a big round of applause!"

"Bravo! Ibrahim! You're the man! You're a hero!"

People call Ibrahim's name until he steps up to the makeshift stage. Annie is the loudest.

Monsieur Pottier gets down from his chair and squeezes Ibrahim's hand between his two. I catch a small grimace on my friend's face. He looks even more terrible when Madame Pottier plants two kisses on each of his cheeks.

"We've got something special for you." Monsieur Pottier cranes his neck and waves to someone in the crowd.

Mademoiselle Moulin makes her way to Monsieur Pottier and waits for all of us to quiet down. "Now," she says. "Monsieur Pottier is right. Ibrahim is a hero. Heroes deserve rewards. We have a special one for a special boy, and I'm now calling a special man: Doug Sweet!"

Why is she calling my father? Besides being a generous Santa, what else has he done that I don't know of? Dad elbows his way to Ibrahim and Mademoiselle Moulin.

"As the most recent member of the Centre d'Assimilation pour Immigrants," he says, "I could see how some people in Château Moines worked hard to improve recent immigrants' lives." My father pauses, searching for the right words. After all, his French is like mine, a work in progress. "Anyway," he goes on. "I knew right away that something was missing, and it became more important after what Ibrahim did." He gets a piece of paper from his shirt pocket, unfolds it, and smoothes it with his hand. He brandishes the paper in the air. "Plans for a soccer field, built in honor of Ibrahim!"

Loud, enthusiastic clapping follows my father's words, and everybody is cheering his announcement. Ibrahim's face breaks into a mechanical smile, but my friend looks as panicked as a rabbit caught in the beams of a car's headlights.

I can't blame him. It's also too much information for me. I owe two people some real apologies, but I have no idea how I can do it. In just two weeks, the father I thought was interested in another woman is a true believer in social justice, and the librarian I believed was seducing my father is in fact some kind of colleague.

Groovy. Just groovy.

47 A FIRST CONCERT

[*Sylvie:*]

Scott's father hugs Ibrahim. Mademoiselle Moulin gives Ibrahim a light kiss on the cheek. Ibrahim looks like he has been struck by lightning. My parents have smiled so much since Elle was found that their faces are distorted into permanent grins. Annie cheers Ibrahim on with loud shouts and screams. Monsieur Leroy and his wife kiss each other. Detective Richard and Troubadour exchange high fives. Garçon lifts his glass to the sky. Elle and Stacey jump up and down. The Colonel taps the ground with his cane and Mémé taps with her foot. Everywhere I look, happy faces smile at each other.

"What are you doing?" I ask Scott when I see him getting his guitar.

He sticks a pick between his teeth. "Playing music."

"Good idea."

"Go get your stuff," he says, searching for his music.

"What?"

He straps his guitar across his chest. "You are a songwriter, right?"

"I try to be."

"And you want to be a singer."

A knot tightens my throat. "Maybe. I don't know."

Scott narrows his eyes. "Really, today you've got a great opportunity to perform."

My legs are as wobbly as melted marshmallows. "I can't. Nobody knows."

"Even better," Scott says. He tunes his guitar. Then he looks me straight in the eyes. "Let's have a concert. Together. We'll play like we've done it at the cabane."

My heart presses on my stomach and my lunch rises to my mouth. On my way to my room, I step over Chocolat, sprawled on the ground. He has also eaten too much. I open my trunk and slide my notebook into my back pocket. The house purrs, sleepy and cozy. I'm so tempted to stay inside, but I figure Scott will look for me.

As a matter of fact, he pokes his head into my room. "You coming or what?"

"I'm scared," I say.

"Good, now come on."

My notebook makes a bulge in my pocket, and I feel the weight of my songs, urging me to let them out and be heard. Yet my stomach does cartwheels when I think of what awaits me outside. Chocolat stretches his paws in his dream, and I give him a small pat on the back. He lets go of a lazy sigh and falls back to sleep.

I stay at the door, unable to step forward. People are sitting or lying on the grass all over our yard. "Green Beach" I think, staring at the people as if I could make them disappear. Papa has opened the parasols and the older people have gathered under them. It smells of dying fire, of warm sun, and of leftover food. "Party Over," I write in my head, hoping it could be true.

"Now!" Scott says, and I obey him, as I did months ago, when I didn't know him and yet found it impossible not to follow him.

He hauls two chairs under the flowering cherry tree. Nobody pays attention to us until Scott strums his guitar. As if on cue, Stacey, Elle, and petit Paul appear.

"He can play anything he wants," Stacey tells petit Paul.

"Anything?" Elle asks Scott. "Really?"

"Your wish is my command, majesty," Scott says, bowing in front of her.

Elle giggles and drops to the ground. Soon all of the kids join her. Then the adults follow, and in no time people have gathered around Scott. Everybody claps.

"A song! A song!"

"What about Elton John?" Scott says.

Everyone gets wild. I know that French people like Elton John, and Scott has made a great choice with "Your Song." Too bad he doesn't play the piano. He's getting real good, and I'm a complete knot when I think of what's coming up next.

"Thank you," Scott says. "And now," he waits for the clapping to calm down, "join me in welcoming an exceptional artist."

People look around, expecting someone to stand up, but nobody moves. I make myself smaller on the grass. *Exceptional! Who is he kidding? Please!*

"Who is it?" Maman asks me, but by now I can only think of one thing: escape.

"Ladies and gentlemen," Scott says. "Sylvie Pottier!"

"You don't play an instrument," Maman says. "You don't sing." She searches for my eyes. "You do?" She sounds surprised and a bit hurt also, but she reaches for my hand that she squeezes once. "Go!" she says.

"Sylvie! Sylvie!" Stacey and Elle shout.

Now that everybody knows it's me, they clap their hands and call my name, too. I have no choice but obey. I feel people staring at me and I don't know how I make my way to Scott.

"You'll pay for that!" I tell him.

"Sure," he says. "*Mesdames, Messieurs,* Sylvie will entertain you with songs from her own repertoire." He backs up, leaving me alone.

Silence falls onto the yard like a curtain on a stage.

I take a deep breath to slow the galloping of the blood inside me. *Well,* I tell myself, *if this is what you want to do with your life, you better give it a start.* I flip my notebook open.

What will I sing? This is crazy. Scott is crazy. But he tunes his guitar and plucks the strings, and I take a deep breath. My voice sounds small and fragile, but with Scott accompanying me, note after note, peace makes its way through me.

When the world is a battlefield
Peace is a bright star of hope.
When the world is at war
Peace starts right here at home.

When the chorus starts for the second time, I step closer to the people sitting at my feet. "Together!" I say, and everybody sings with me.

One song follows another, and before I know it I've sung my most favorite songs.

"*Une autre! Une autre!*" Elle and Stacey shout. They are my biggest fans. But I also see Annie cupping her hands around her mouth, asking for another song.

The sun is vanishing behind the trees, and it's not as warm anymore. The Colonel drapes his jacket on Mémé's shoulders. I can think of only one song to end my performance. I wrote it after Scott and I found la cabane.

The sun sets on the horizon,
Like a curtain on a stage,
Fold after fold,
Until night brings

Peace and silence on earth,
Hope and harmony on us.

The notes from Scott's guitar match my words. The music he plays is what my feelings sound like. Seconds after we are finished, music still lingers in the air, and nobody moves. I'm afraid to breathe and break the magic of the moment. Even Chocolat, who has woken up and joined us, is quiet, the wagging of his tail only sign of his enthusiasm.

Then everybody cheers and rushes to congratulate me. Chocolat bounds to me, and we are surrounded by a dozen of kids, shouting that I'm the best. Then they gallop to the dessert table. I feel too wired to eat anything. Music fills every cell of my body with energy and lifts my soul up to the sky.

"Beautiful!" Mademoiselle Moulin says, joining her hands, prayer-like. "I'm so proud of you. You truly are an artist."

"Isn't she amazing?" Mémé says, tossing her hair back. She smiles and pride lights her face. "*Ma belle,* your writing is exceptional, isn't it, Colonel?"

He straightens the jacket around Mémé's shoulders. "Songs, songs, *pfft,*" he says, but his lips curl up when he adds, "Talent is precious. Don't waste it. Keep writing."

"I knew there were lots of great words in there," Monsieur Leroy says, tapping the top of my head. "Keep up the good work, Sylvie!"

Compliments wrap themselves around me like a silky scarf, keeping me warm yet free and light.

"Well, well," Annie says, a half smile stretching her lips. "Who would have known?" She slams her body against mine. "Let's hug like the Americans," she says with a laugh. She pulls away a little. "Really cool," she says. "You're good."

I catch a glimpse of my parents walking toward me. "I'd better leave you alone," Annie says and she saunters away.

Papa clears his throat. "Why didn't you tell us that you write songs?"

Because words are harder for me to say than to write, I think.

"We love songs," Maman says.

"Don't think that because we don't listen to the same kind of music," Papa adds, "we don't like music."

Maman searches my eyes. "I had no idea you had such talent," she says. "I'm so proud of you, *mon chou*."

"I am too, *ma puce*." Papa kisses the top of my head.

And for once, it doesn't bother me to be my mother's pastry puff and my father's flea. A pastry puff is small but sweet, and a flea is annoying but tiny. Maybe that's why they nicknamed me *chou* and *puce*. No matter what, I'll be their sweet little girl, but today I've shown them what the sweet little girl is capable of, and I have to finish the job.

"I want to be a songwriter when I grow up," I say. "Maybe a singer, too."

My parents look at each other and then at me. "You can be whoever you want," Maman says.

"And I want to live in Paris," I go on.

"I will miss you when you leave home, but I won't stop you," Maman says.

Papa nods, sucking on his lower lip. "I fully agree," he says. And then he waves Scott over. "Good music, son," he says in a professional tone that makes me smile.

Scott's cheeks are red with embarrassment. "*Merci, monsieur,*" he says.

"Now, Denis," Maman says, grabbing my father's hand. "We've got some cleanup to do." Papa pretends to be offended, but his eyes twinkle.

As soon as my parents are out of sight, Scott hugs me. "You're far out," he says.

I squirm to look up at him, but my movement brings my lips to his cheek. *Too late,* I think, and I kiss him right there.

"Now, that you live in France," I say. "It's time you gave up your weird embraces for kisses."

Scott blushes, but he kisses me back. "Happy?" he says.

He has no idea.

48 CHANGE

[*Scott:*]

Sylvie's kiss burns my skin, but in a really good way. I stick my guitar in its case, close it shut, and sit on the ground. The cool grass tickles my bare feet. All around me, kids, loaded with sugar and excitement, bump into each other, laughing and screaming.

Stacey and Elle drag a big trash bag behind them like an opened parachute. Brigitte and a boy I haven't noticed until now are stuffing dirty plates, cups, and napkins inside the bag. The little girls pretend to run away and the boy chases them, giggling like a little kid although he's two heads taller than me.

"Good job, Jacques!" Brigitte says, even though the boy has missed the bag and left dirty plates and balled napkins behind.

She turns on her heels and sees me. First she looks away, but changes her mind and walks toward me. I look down at my feet, embarrassed that she saw me observing her and whoever Jacques is.

"I feel sorry for this boy," I say.

"Why would you?" Brigitte sits next to me. She cups her hands around her knees. "He lives in Paris, in a beautiful place."

I get a glimpse of Jacques traipsing behind Elle and Stacey. "That's cool," I say.

"And he has tons of friends." Brigitte has a small laugh. "Very unique, like him."

I dig the grass with my toes, looking ahead. Jacques has caught up with Elle and Stacey, and the three of them are trying to fit the bulging bag in the garbage can.

"He got very sick," Brigitte says, when we've been quiet for the longest time. "He was only a few days old. My mother blamed herself, my father blamed himself, and when they couldn't stand to blame themselves anymore, they sent Jacques away and had me." She kicks my guitar case with her heel. "I'm the only girl around who has an older brother who acts like a baby. Until now I wouldn't have told anyone." She searches for my eyes. "But everything is different since you came."

I don't know if different is always good, so I dig the ground a little deeper until I hit a rock. "Ouch!" I rub my big toe.

"You okay?" Brigitte brushes her hair away from her face and inspects my foot like a nurse. "You don't need an amputation," she declares with a small smile.

She points at Jacques and the girls, rolling on the grass. "I told my parents that Jacques could be happy here. They agreed we could give it a try." She gives me a real smile. "That peace rally thing you organized, you know, it really changed everything. Now people are talking to each other like they never did before."

A cool breeze falls on the yard, and more people are saying their goodbyes. Splashes of color, sounds of laughter, and a word here and there come to me, but I don't know what people are talking about. The yard looks like a painting by this French artist, Renoir, the one who painted scenes of picnics along the French rivers.

Next to me Brigitte is quiet, and I think of what she just said, of how my arriving in Château Moines has changed things. Impossible. How could a boy like me, a foreigner, have done anything to a town that has a castle from the Middle Ages and a rotten drawbridge? "That's you," I tell Brigitte. "All of you have changed everything."

"Really, Scott, you are too humble," she says with a laugh.

I elbow her. "Shut up!"

She elbows me back. "Never!" she says with another laugh as she walks away.

Mademoiselle Moulin returns from her car with a stack of records. "Music!" she calls.

Sylvie gets her record player and an extension cord and sets them up in the yard.

"Chicago?" Dad suggests.

"A horn section is definitely a must for such a day," Troubadour says.

Soon trumpets and saxophones fill the night with their smooth and round sounds. The sky above us has turned the color of Monsieur Leroy's ink pen. Stars shoot through the darkness, and I squeeze Mom's earring in my pocket. I don't need the stars to remind me of her stellar love or to know that she would be happy to see me happy tonight.

49   TRUTH OR DARE

[*Sylvie:*]

Papa gathers some wood and lights a match. The smoke makes us cough. Small flames dance in the air. We all crowd around the fire, listening to the music and the snapping of the wood. Scott sits across from me. His kiss lingers on my skin, and I smile from inside and out.

"Does anyone care for a game?" Mémé suggests, when the record stops at the end of its track.

"Let's play truth or dare!" Annie says, jumping to her feet.

"Count me out," Scott says, warming his hands above the fire.

"I'll take your spot, then." Mémé pulls up two chairs for the Colonel and for her.

I don't know if it's the night falling like a soft blanket, my first concert, or my first kiss on Scott's cheek that gives me unexpected guts.

"Mémé," I say. "Truth or dare?"

My grandmother looks up at me, and when our eyes meet, she knows I'm up to something. "Truth," she says on an even tone.

I pick a twig and toy with it. "Is it true that Hollywood Follies took the place of a store called Le Petit Paris that had been closed for years?"

Mémé shoots a definitive, "True."

Papa clears his throat, and all eyes turn to him. "Truth or dare?" he asks Mémé.

Mémé clicks her tongue. "Dare."

"Dare you to tell us the story of Le Petit Paris?"

The twig snaps between my hands. Mémé holds Papa's gaze and she takes a deep breath.

"Le Petit Paris," she says, "was more than a store to everyone who grew up here. The owners dressed all of us for every special occasion. Le Petit Paris was a symbol." She pauses as if she wanted all of us of to imagine the store. "The owners had a daughter named Marie, and she had always said she would go to Paris someday."

Maman's bitter laugh interrupts Mémé. "She didn't want to have anything to do with our little town," she says. "As she grew up, she didn't care for the friends she had anymore and left as soon as she finished high school to pursue whatever dreams she had. When her parents died, we all knew that only Marie could change the fate of the store. But she didn't. We never heard of her again. The store closed and remained closed for more than twenty years until someone bought it and opened some other store."

Maman shoots a dark look at Scott's father. I feel terrible: Why is she blaming him for a past he doesn't know, for a part of her life he has nothing to do with?

"I think it's wonderful that the store was given another life," Mémé says, and she sends a warm and kind smile in direction of Scott's father, who nods a polite thank-you.

"I agree," Garçon says. "It's also great that it's so different from Le Petit Paris. I bet Marie would love it."

"Haven't you ever thought," Maman says in a shaking voice, "that someone here would have liked to take over the store? But it was never for sale." She points at Papa. "You know that Marie kept it only to prove to us that a stranger was more interesting than any of us!"

"Game over!" Papa says, jumping to his feet.

Everyone falls silent. Mémé rushes to Maman and wraps her arm around her shoulders.

"Sometimes," Mémé says, "things happen, and they leave an open wound that never heals well."

"It has nothing to do with you, Doug," Papa says in a low voice. He looks up, searching for Scott's father's eyes. "All of us are glad that you moved here and gave a second chance to a store that had been neglected for too long."

I'm so confused. What are Mémé and Papa talking about? Why is Maman so upset? About a store she dreamed to open and couldn't, because a girl she didn't like didn't sell it?

Scott's father stands up, interrupting my thoughts. He rubs his hands above the dancing flames of the campfire.

"I'm sorry you feel that way," he says. "I'm sure that if Marie had known how much Le Petit Paris meant to you, she would have considered things another way."

"How would you know?" Maman meets his eyes. "How would you know better than I know?" The freezing tone of her voice slices through the night.

"Because," Scott's father says, "I married Marie and spent the happiest years of my life with her."

Silence follows his words, as if the air itself was holding its breath. My mother's face is the color of the cinders around the fire. I'm trying to gather clearer thoughts while Scott is keeping his eyes on the ground.

Scott's father clears his voice. "I'm the only reason why Marie didn't return to Château Moines when her parents passed away." We are all suspended on his words. "We had met in Paris and she followed me to California, where we got married. Two years ago, she was diagnosed with terminal cancer and passed away last year. What you don't know is that she left me and our children Le Petit Paris to fulfill our dream to open a store together." His voice catches in his throat, and everyone keeps silent.

When Maman makes her way to him, she takes tiny steps as if his confession was sinking deep inside her, weighing her down. "*Je suis désolée*," she says between sobs. "I am so sorry for what I said."

I wonder if Scott's father can forgive my mother's harsh words.

Papa's voice startles us. "I must add something," he says, "so my wife Simone can be at peace." He pauses, and the only sound is the sputtering of the wood in the fire pit. "I was Simone's steady boyfriend all through high school," Papa says. "But right after we got our high school diplomas, she broke up with me because I danced with Marie on Bastille Day."

One by one, the reasons why my mother couldn't bring herself to accept the Hollywood Follies make sense. Yet it's awful to hear the truth from my father, and I don't dare look up, embarrassed to meet Scott's eyes.

"Marie had always said she would leave Château Moines," Papa goes on. "And she did. A few years later, I married the love of my life and I never saw Marie again."

The tapping sound of a cane makes us turn toward the Colonel. "These children," he says, pointing at us, "don't need grown-up stories. What they need is a place to live their own stories." He turns to Mémé. "Do you remember my little house in the forest?"

Mémé rolls her eyes. "I'm not that old! Of course I remember." Her dimples smile when she adds, "But you don't remember where your little house is, if I'm correct."

"I haven't really looked for it," the Colonel says.

"Anyway, I decided to give it to the children of Château Moines. If they can find it, that is."

"A little house!" Stacey and Elle jump to their feet. "Cool! Merci, Colonel!"

"*Pfft*," the Colonel says with a wave of his cane.

Elle peeks at Scott and then at me. A huge smile splashes across her face. I wag my finger and Chocolat wags his tail.

"Music, anyone?" Troubadour puts on Genesis, and Peter Gabriel's smooth voice rocks the night.

"What kind of picnic is this?" Annie says, without looking at me. "It's like going to confession. On top of everything, you won't guess what my foster parents want to do."

"I've had enough surprises for one day," I say.

"Right." She keeps quiet. "They want to adopt me." And before I get a chance to say anything, she adds in a quick, nervous tone, "Have you heard anything more stupid?"

"I think it's a *chouette* idea," Scott says, right behind us. He squeezes between Annie and me. "They love you."

"Love is so overrated," Annie says, but her voice turns mellow.

"They really love you," Scott repeats.

"So I should say yes?"

"Definitely," I say.

"Absolutely," Scott says.

Annie starts a silly dance around us. "I already did!"

We laugh as we watch her skipping away, blowing us goodbye kisses.

"Scott," I say as a mix of embarrassment and relief washes over me. "I'm sorry about your mom and I feel terrible about mine."

Scott shrugs. "Your mom had no idea. Besides she had excuses."

I look up at the sky. One by one, stars have appeared while we spoke. "Pick one for your maman," I whisper. "So you can see her every night in the French sky."

"I told you I quit believing in stuff like that after she died," Scott says, but I catch him glancing at the sky, dark like a fading bruise. A slow smile grows on his lips. "In a way," he says, "we are related."

I make a face. "Because my father…" I don't even want to go there.

"Not that!" With a real grin, he says, "Without the store, I wouldn't have moved to France."

"It's incredible that we met because of a store," I say. "But it doesn't make us cousins or anything like that, right?"

Scott smiles his Hollywood smile. "That's the best part. Related, but not relatives."

His hand wraps around my wrist and my skin tingles all over my body. I slip my hand into his and we kiss for the second time today.

Only this time not on the cheeks.

50 LE PETIT PARIS IS ALIVE

[*Scott:*]

Chocolat trots over; his tail makes an excited *swish, swish* sound. He brushes against my leg, over and over again, and I think dogs are lucky to show their love without saying anything. Around me, the yard buzzes with laughter, conversation, and crickets.

Nobody notices me when I leave and close the gate behind me. The streets are so quiet that I only hear the flip-flop sound of my sandals on the sidewalk. I don't want to look up, but I know that high in the sky the stars keep showing off their beauty. I'm now living 6,000 miles away from home, with one earring to remind me of my mother. Yet, despite her absence and the endless war going on in Vietnam, a feeling of calm is inching its way through me. In a strange and unexpected way, I belong here. I have made friends and even have had my first real kiss.

Without noticing it, I've reached Hollywood Follies. Dad has locked the entrance, so I get in through the apartment. The lights are off inside the store, and I fumble around the racks of clothes. I sit on Dad's swiveling chair and spin until I get dizzy and feel like throwing up.

"You just had too much good food, too much wind and air, too much fun," Mom used to say when I felt light-headed after a long day on the beach. Her voice sounds so close, so real, that I expect to see her.

And besides her voice, I hear voices of the past, when Hollywood Follies was Le Petit Paris, and when a little French girl was wandering along the aisles of the only clothing store in Château Moines, dreaming about leaving her small town for Paris someday.

I'm back to the starting point, to the place that made me, long before anyone knew I would exist, to the store that was part of my mother's life and is now part of mine. We left Santa Monica, where Mom haunted every street, every stretch of the beach, until we couldn't breathe. We came to Château Moines, and I thought we would leave Mom far behind.

But here we are, in the very same store that saw her cry and laugh. Her smile is drawn on the walls and her words are printed on the store's awning.

From now on Le Petit Paris lives through Hollywood Follies, as if Mom had never left.
And I am finding peace.

ACKNOWLEDGMENTS

My writing group, and especially Joan, read the manuscript at different stages.

Isabelle Stein copy-edited the last version.

Jennifer Zemanek designed and realized the cover.

My husband formatted the printed book and the e-book.

My children introduced me to many books and still do.

Bloggers encouraged me through kind comments and shared experiences.

Writers that I read in French or in English remain my daily companions through my life and writing journey.

To each of you: Thank you

A FEW WORDS FROM THE AUTHOR

Although *Chronicles From Château Moines* is a work of fiction, the cultural, social and historical backgrounds of the early '70s in France and the USA inspired the novel.

Music

Music plays a big role in teenagers' lives, regardless of the period of time and the country. The music both Sylvie and Scott like illustrates the musical melting pot of the early '70s.

Throughout *Chronicles From Château Moines,* the following bands, songs and singers are cited:

- "Surfin' USA" - song and album 1963, by American rock band the Beach Boys
- "Mrs. Robinson" - song from album Bookends 1968, by American pop/folk music duo Paul Simon and Art Garfunkel
- "L'Amérique" - song from album La Fleur aux Dents 1970, by French singer Joe Dassin
- "Let it be" - song and album 1970, by British rock band the Beatles
- "The 59th Street Bridge Song (*Feelin'*

Groovy)"- song from album Parsley, Sage, Rosemary and Thyme 1966, by Simon and Garfunkel

- "Try Just a Little Bit Harder"- song from album I Got Dem Ol' Kozmic Blues Again Mama! 1969, by American singer, songwriter Janis Joplin
- "25 or 6 to 4" - song and album 1970, by American rock, jazz, fusion band Chicago
- "I Am a Rock" - song from album Sounds of Silence 1966, by Simon and Garfunkel
- "We Can Work it Out" - song released as a double-A sided with Day Tripper in 1965, by the Beatles
- "Gimme Shelter"- song from album Let it Bleed 1969, by British rock band the Rolling Stones
- "Black Magic Woman" - song written by Peter Green that first appeared as a Fleetwood Mac single in various countries in 1968, rearranged by the Latin-influenced rock band Santana and released on the album Abraxas in 1970
- "Bridge over Troubled Water"- song and album 1970, final studio album by Simon and Garfunkel.
- "Last Night I Had the Strangest Dream"- song written by Ed McCurdy in 1950 that became one the anthems of the anti-war

era, performed by John Denver on April 14, 1971 at a peace march in Washington D.C.

- "Blowin' in the Wind"- song from album The Freewheelin' Bob Dylan 1963, by the American singer, songwriter Bob Dylan. The folk music trio Peter, Paul and Mary released a successful version three weeks later

- "Stop the War Now!"- song from album the Very Best of Edwin Starr 1971, by American soul music singer Edwin Starr

- "Your Song"- song from album Elton John 1970, by British rock, pop singer Elton John

Also mentioned are the following artists:

- Carol King, American singer and songwriter

- Francoise Hardy, French singer and songwriter

- Joan Baez, American folk singer and songwriter

- These three artists began their successful, prolific and enduring careers in the '60s.

- Janis Joplin, American singer and songwriter, rose to fame in the late '60s. She died on October 4, 1970.

- Jimmy Hendrix, American musician,

singer, and songwriter. He died on Sept. 18, 1970.

- The Poppys, a French children band whose songs originated from the hippie and anti-war movements of the late '60s early '70s. The original band ended in 1978.

Fashion

Scott wears Levi's, Hang Ten shirts, Birkenstock, Huarache, and flip-flops. He carries his textbooks in a backpack adorned with peace buttons while Sylvie dreams of her first pair of Levi's and her own army backpack. Brigitte wears tight sweaters, flared jeans and platform shoes. Annie wears a green vinyl jacket.

In the early '70s French and American teenagers alike wore a mix of hippie-style and pre disco clothes.

While French teens embraced the American clothes, wearing clothes that embodied rebellion and freedom, their parents were more critical. Jeans, in particular, represented a lifestyle that some French conservatives associated with excessive freedom. In some schools, private Catholic school in particular, French girls weren't allowed to wear pants and makeup.

French teens would have loved a boutique like Hollywood Follies and in the early '70s such stores started to open in small towns while Paris and large

French cities offered more shopping opportunities.

Immigration in France in 1970

After World War II, Algerian, Moroccan, Tunisian, and Portuguese workers came to France to help rebuild the country. Thanks to the American Marshall Plan, Western Europe will, in only a few years, rebound from the devastation of war. Starting in the early '50s the immigrants were mostly young single men from the Maghreb (Algeria, Morocco, Tunisia) who came to work in the French factories. They lived on the outskirts of the cities and would later be joined by their families. The French economic growth will slow down in the early '70s, leading to a rigorous control of work immigration.

Despite France's long immigration history, some residents of fictional Château Moines struggle to accept the new comers who settle in their little town. What happens in the story reflects how the French were caught between suspicion and empathy.

The Vietnam War

The Vietnam War is the name of the conflict that will last from 1954 to 1975. The conflict started after the French Indochina (the French colonies of the territory now occupied by Cambodia, Laos, and

Vietnam) won its independence, following one hundred years of French colonial presence.

The prolonged war between the communist armies of North Vietnam, supported by the Chinese, and the armies of South Vietnam, supported by the United States, will be the most significant and deathly conflict during the Cold War.

Starting in the late '60s and rising in the early '70s a majority of Americans disapproved of their country's involvement in Vietnam. Millions voiced their opposition to the war through massive protests and peace walks.

In *Chronicles From Château Moines*, Scott is more politically engaged than Sylvie. His attitude reflects the American growing opposition to the Vietnam War.

However, popular opposition to war, to violence in general, and to the excessive power of governments marked the '70s in both France and the USA.

Other Cultural, Social and Historical Facts

- Neil Armstrong was an American astronaut, military pilot, and educator. On July 20, 1969 he became the first man to walk on the moon.
- The Concorde plane was the result of a joint venture between France and the

United Kingdom. The first Concorde was flown in 1969. Commercial flights started on January 21, 1976 and ended on October 14, 2003.

- The Brady Bunch is an American sitcom that originally aired from September 26, 1969 to March 8, 1974. The series revolved around a large blended family, which included six children.

- Mademoiselle Âge Tendre, French magazine inspired by the American magazine Seventeen, was created for teenage girls. The magazine was launched in the fall 1964 and its publication ended in 1974.

- Mardi Gras is a French celebration tied to the Catholic calendar. It is celebrated forty-seven days before Easter, on the Tuesday before Ash Wednesday, which marks the beginning of Lent. On this festive day French people wear costumes and eat crepes and beignets. In the USA Mardi Gras is mostly celebrated in Louisiana and especially in the French Quarter in New Orleans.

- George Pompidou was President of France between 1969 and 1974. He died while being President on April 2, 1974.

- Richard Nixon was President of the United States of America between 1969 and 1974. He died on April 22, 1994.

- Charles de Gaulle was a French general who led the Free French Forces during World War II. He was the President of France from 1959 to 1969. He died on November 9, 1970.

- May 8 commemorates the date when the World War II Allies officially accepted the unconditional surrender of the armed forces of Nazi Germany and also the end of Hitler's Third Reich, consequently ending the war in Europe.

- In many parts of the world the year 1968 was marked by popular protests against military, capitalist, and bureaucratic elites.

- In the United States these protests marked a turning point for the Civil Rights Movement.

- In France university students joined forces with millions of workers. For a few days during the month of May violence exploded in Paris and big cities in such a way that the movement seemed able to overthrow the government.

Evelyne Holingue was born and raised in France. Now she lives with her family in the United States. Through her writing she shares her affection for her two favorite countries. In this novel, she also shares a few of her favorite songs that she sings at the top of her lungs when alone.

Find Evelyne at www.evelyneholingue.com

15972695R00193

Made in the USA
San Bernardino, CA
12 October 2014